Cousin Mary

Mrs. Oliphant

Cousin Mary

The present edition is a reproduction of previous publication of this classic work. Minor typographical errors may have been corrected without note; however, for an authentic reading experience the spelling, punctuation, and capitalization have been retained from the original text.

ISBN: 978-1-63637-434-5

CONTENTS

CHAPTER I

ONLY MARY

THE Prescotts of Horton had been a powerful family in their day. Their house still was more in accordance with their past greatness than with the mediocrity of their fortune at the period of their history which has first to be indicated to the reader. They were no longer in the first rank in their county, but had settled down by degrees without any great fall, into the position of ordinary squires: that is to say, their fall had happened a hundred and fifty years before, in the time of that unhappy attempt to subvert the government established by the Revolution, which is known as the "Fifteen." The Prescott of that period had joined the rebellion, if rebellion it could be called, and had escaped with his life at its disastrous conclusion. His son had secured a portion of the family belongings, but never had been able to regain the wealth or the position of his forefathers; and since then the family had remained humble but proud, thinking a great deal of themselves, but not thought quite so much of by their neighbours—a family not clever, nor any way distinguished, yet furnishing its quota of stout soldiers and respectable clergymen, with now and then a lawyer or two, to the service of the state.

The elder brother, the Squire, had been generally a dullish, goodish sort of man, doing his duty fairly well, fairly kind to his younger brothers and sisters, keeping up the ancestral house as well as he could on means not great enough for any splendour, and giving more or less a home to the scattered members of his family. The great advantage of those much abused laws of primogeniture, entail, or whatever else they may be which fix the succession in one member of a family, is this—that they are far more apt to keep up a central point, a family home, than any other arrangement yet discovered. When all share alike, no one has any particular claim upon the others, and ancestral homes, like all other primitive regulations for preserving the sacred nucleus of the family, cease to be.

The younger Prescott brothers went off to seek their fortunes in every generation; the elder always kept up the house. It depended upon his character, and perhaps still more on that of his wife, whether this home was or was not a kindly one, but still it was always there; a possible shelter in all circumstances, a perpetual court of appeal against the injustices of the world.

1

I have not space enough here to describe the old house, which was much too great for the income and pretensions of the present occupant. It was a great house, partly Elizabethan, with additions in later days, with two great wings, in one of which was a fine portrait gallery, while the other contained the show apartments of the house, a suite of rooms which were quite worthy to have been occupied by a king, though fact compels us to add that royalty had made but a very slight use of them. King Charles, in one of his hasty rides in the midst of his troubled career, had paused to eat a morsel in the hall, and to wash his royal hands in a dressing-room. This was all, but it was something, and the rooms were beautiful with their faded furniture and heavy old hangings and tapestries, and chairs covered with embroidered work. All this was very much faded, and kept with difficulty from falling to pieces; but it was very imposing, and strangers came from all quarters to see the house. The pictures in the gallery were all portraits now, though it was a tradition that there had once been several old Masters which were sold in the troubles, but of which the frames still remained, blankly filled up by pieces of old brocade, in themselves a sight to see. Some even of the portraits, especially those which had been painted by famous masters, had disappeared too, so that the importance of the gallery in point of art was small.

These remains of glory past were separate from the living part of the house. They were kept in order, and shown to strangers, a point of family pride which every Prescott held to be essential. But the existing Prescotts lived in the centre part of the house, which was too large for them, with its great hall and the other beautiful rooms, so airy and spacious, which were the creation of a generation which did not fear expense and loved space. The fine wainscoted room which was used as the dining-room in modern days, accommodated thirty people easily at dinner, whereas the Prescotts numbered but six, and seldom had company. The drawing-room was still larger, with noble broad bay windows, each as big as a modern room. To furnish all this, it may be supposed, was no trifle; and the furniture was shabby; what was old, faded; what was new, not half good enough for the natural splendour of the place. Nevertheless, new and old together harmonised somehow by mere use and wont, and the general appearance was that of a mingled humility and pride, like the character of the family, which thought such great things of itself and yet was able to do only little things and occupy a small position in the world.

This family consisted of six persons, as has been said—the

2

Squire and his wife; the eldest son, who was very far from clever, who was, indeed, sometimes considered to be "not all there," a mild, long young man, with an elongated, melancholy visage, not unlike that of the tragic monarch whose passing visit had given a historical association to the house. His name was not a romantic one; it was plain John, according to the habit of the house. He was very mild in all his tastes; good so far as a person, so neutral-tinted could be called good; kind, disturbing nobody, ready to do almost anything that was asked of him, so long as it was asked with due regard to his dignity—but as thoroughly aware of his importance as a Prescott, and the eldest son, as if he had possessed all the brains of the house. Then there were two sisters, no longer very young, but who had not yet renounced the rôle of youth, and who were always called "the girls," according to general family usage.

Last of all was Percival, the soldier, the youngest, the prodigal, the spendthrift, the clever one, the beloved of the house. All these names do not mean that there was anything bad about Percy—quite the reverse. His gaiety made the house bright, his laugh rang through all the great rooms and woke cheerful echoes. Money trickled through his fingers he could not tell how, but he did no particular harm with it. The worst was that he was generally away from home with his regiment, and when he came home, though it was a delight to look forward to, and did everybody good, Mr. Prescott was always awfully conscious that for this happiness there would certainly be a good deal to pay. "That is all very well, my dear," he would say to his wife, "so long as I live: but when John is master poor Percy will find out the difference." "Ah, John!" Mrs. Prescott would answer, with a sigh, wondering in her heart who John's wife would be, thinking what a good thing it would be if he were not to marry, feeling sure that whoever married him would be the future ruler of Horton. That was the danger that lay in her gallant Percy's way.

This accounts for five people, and I have said there were six. The last was only Mary. The other members of the family would have thought it quite unnecessary to give any further description of her. She was the one who did all manner of little errands in the house, and little offices. She arranged the flowers; if Anna wanted something upstairs it was Mary who ran to fetch it; if Sophie left anything in the garden, or on one of the tables in the hall, Mary always knew where to find it. She fetched Mr. Prescott the newspaper he had left about, and found her aunt's spectacles, and got John his hat, which he always forgot when he was going out. When Percy was at home she did all sorts of commissions for him; even the old housekeeper gave her messages and things to carry.

"Just put this in the drawing-room, Miss Mary, my dear," or, "Will you take these books to Miss Anna?" was what Mrs. Beesly said half-a-dozen times a day. They meant no harm whatever, and did not oppress her, or ill-use her, or neglect her, or do any of the things which are supposed to be done to a little dependent orphan in her uncle's house. Perhaps they may have been said to have neglected her, but not of any evil intent.

They meant no harm; she was only Mary: there was no particular reason that anybody knew of for thinking of her, or putting anybody out of their way on her account. She was a child in the opinion of all the others, even of "the girls." She was not included in that term. She was not even advanced to the rank of one of the girls. She was only Mary. She had never been whipped, or scolded, or put in dark closets, or set to hard tasks all her life. It is true that Anna's and Sophie's old dresses were very often "made down" for her: but that would have happened all the same had she been Anna's and Sophie's sister. Her life was happy enough; she had a share of everything that was going; and it never had occurred to her that she should be made of any particular account.

In her own mind, as well as in the conviction of the whole household, she was only Mary. She was a quiet little thing, but always cheerful, ready to talk when any one wanted to talk, or to play her little pieces when asked for them, or to be silent like a little mouse when there was no need for such vanities. She took herself as easily as the others took her, making no sort of pretension. Nor did she feel wronged, or offended, or slighted, as some might have done. She was only Mary, not Miss Prescott of Horton, as both the girls were. She was not even a Prescott, only a sister's daughter, an unconsidered trifle in the feminine line. Her whole life was pitched in this minor key, but it was not at all an unhappy little life at her age, for she was barely twenty. It had not yet begun to matter very much that she was a first object to nobody. As a matter of fact, everything was perfectly natural about her, and she had never found that things might be brighter, or that she really had any aspiration after a more individual life.

She had an uncle at the Rectory as well as at the Hall, but there were no young people in the clerical house. This was how things stood with the Prescotts and Mary Burnet, when the new curate arrived, of whom Uncle Hugh at the Rectory had heard so very good an account. Uncle Hugh was a very conscientious clergyman. He liked to keep the parish in thoroughly good working order, but if truth must be told he preferred that some one else should do the work for him. He had the very best recommendations with the new curate. He was hard-working, he

4

was moderate, not too much of a ritualist, and yet a very good Churchman, and a man who socially took nothing upon him; a retiring, modest young man. The Rector was most fortunate in getting a curate like Mr. Asquith, everybody said.

CHAPTER II

ONLY THE CURATE

A CURATE is a very useful member of the Church militant. He is the stuff out of which all its more dignified functionaries are made; and he does a great deal of the hard work, with a very limited proportion of the pay. But notwithstanding all this, he has a great deal to put up with in the way of snubs from his superiors, and indifference from the public, who accept his services often without prizing them very much. He has compensation in his youth, which makes him acceptable to the younger and fairer portion of the flock, and in his hopes of better things, as well as, no doubt, to leave pleasantry apart, in the satisfaction of performing important duties, and doing the sacred work to which he has dedicated himself.

Mr. Asquith, the new curate at Horton, had, however, but few of the compensations. There was a very small number of young ladies in the parish, and he was a young man who did not give himself to croquet or archery, or any of the gentle games then in vogue; for the period of which I speak was before the invention of lawn tennis. To none of these things did he incline. He was ready to tramp along the country roads in dust or in mud to carry consolation to any poor sick-bed. He was never tired with examining schools, catechizing children, conducting little cottage services; for those were the days when a high ritual was unusual, and daily prayers were rare in the churches. He would even interest himself in the village cricket, if need was, though awkwardly, and not in a way which impressed the rustic eleven. As for the minor organisations of the parish, the savings-banks, the clothing clubs, the lending library, they had no existence until he came.

The Rector frankly thought them quiet unnecessary; and Mrs. Prescott was of opinion that to set them a-going was a dangerous thing, and might put such a burden upon the next curate who should succeed Mr. Asquith as that problematical individual might not care to bear; and of course, she added, nobody could expect the Rector himself to be charged with the fatigue of keeping all these new-fangled institutions up.

Mr. Asquith paid little attention to these remonstrances. So long as he had permission to do what he thought right, even if it were only a formal permission, he was satisfied: and he went on working among his poor people, with the greatest indifference to any of those solaces, in the way of society and the making of friends, which are generally supposed to sweeten the lot of his class. He said "Bother!" when he was told that he was expected to be on certain occasions a guest at the Rectory; and he said "What a bore!" when he was invited to dine at the Hall. None of these delights tempted him. When John Prescott called on him, as in duty bound, he found the curate busy among calculations, planning out one of those village charities which were wanting in Horton, and rather abstracted and preoccupied—dull, John said, who was himself the dullest of men.

"I said we might perhaps let him have a day's thooting now and again," said John, who lisped a little.

"And what did he say to that?" said Anna; for indeed the girls were rather interested, and wanted to know what sort of person the new curate was.

"He thook his head," said John; "and so he did when I asked if he was fond of croquet. And then I thaid, was he musical?"

"I hope he is musical," said Sophie, "a violin would be such an addition. What did he say when you asked him that?"

"He thook his head again," answered John.

"Oh, what a horrid man!"

"No, he's not a horrid man; he's a good fellow; but he'th dull—he'th dull," said John, with emphasis; it was when he wanted to be emphatic that he lisped most. And as John was very dull himself, the sisters concluded, not unreasonably, that the man in whom he discovered that quality must be dull indeed.

Mary, who was in the room, listened with some curiosity, too, though she took no part in the conversation; and she was much amused to think that in the world, and even in the parish, there could thus be a duller man than John. Not that she was contemptuous of John for his dulness. She liked him almost the best of the family. He was tiresome, to be sure; if you were thrown upon him for society, it would not be cheerful society; but then you were never thrown upon John—there was always somebody else to talk, and show a little interest. And that he was tiresome was the worst that could be said of him. He never forced his dulness upon any one, as some do. He never wanted to be talked to, or amused, or taken any notice of. His temper was as even, and the grey atmosphere about him as tranquil as heart could desire. He was not clever, but he never gave any trouble, and he could even be very kind when it came into his head.

"Ah, well," said Sophie, "it cannot be helped. A new man might have been an acquisition. He might have taught us some of

7

the new rules for croquet, or he might have played a new instrument, or he might have sung. But it's clear, from what John says, that he's only the curate, and there's nothing more to say."

"I suppose," said Anna, "he must be asked to dinner all the same."

But though they did this only as a matter of duty, they would all have been extremely astonished, not to say offended, had they known that he said "What a bore!" on receiving the invitation. He was at that moment very much occupied about all the new things that he was setting up, altogether indifferent to the consideration that the next curate might not be of his way of thinking and might feel it a burden. Mr. Asquith, however, never spoke of the possibility of a change, but seemed to think that there never would be any other curate. He looked as though he meant to go on forever bringing all his schemes to perfection. The Rector could only afford to give him £100 a year and the use of the cottage in which the curates always lived, with the very barest furniture—merely what was necessary. But Mr. Asquith did not seem to think either of the small stipend or the bare lodgings; he seemed only to think of the work which he made so unnecessarily hard for himself. And presently he was so absorbed in this work, and found so many things to do, and set so many things going which nobody but himself took any interest in, that he fell almost out of the knowledge of the more important persons in the parish. They went their way, which was the old-established, correct way for gentlefolks in a country parish to go, in which they had gone long before he appeared, and would most likely go long after he had disappeared; and he went his, which was novel and new-fangled, and on the whole not a way approved of by the best people. And though the parish was quite small, and you would have supposed that all the educated persons belonging to the upper classes in it must have jostled each other every day, the fact was that they went on in parallel lines, as it were, without ever seeing each other.

He went to the Rectory now and then, of course, as in duty bound, but otherwise, when he was seen passing any of the chief houses in the place, and a chance visitor asked who he was, "Oh, it is only the curate," was always the answer in Horton. This was really almost all that any one knew of him.

As a matter of fact, the Rector knew more, and all the world might have known what his antecedents were. He was a man from the North, the son of one of those sturdy small proprietors who are called statesmen in Cumberland, or were called so in former times—born upon his own paternal acres in a house which had belonged to his family for generations, and thus possessing many

8

of the advantages of ancient lineage, though his was not what is called gentle blood. He had won a scholarship at Oxford, and had made his way through the university without, however, gaining any of those social advantages which, in the eyes of many people, are the chief recommendations of these homes of learning. He had not "made friends." He had settled himself to his work there with the same gravity as at Horton, and thought the finest "wines" and the best company a bore. His talents did not lie in that way. He had no genius for acquaintance, and though he liked the river very well for relaxation, he never could be persuaded to make a business of it, as the boating men did, or, indeed, to "go in" for anything except his work. And even in his work he was not brilliant. His college set no high hopes on his head. He made his way quite quietly, unobserved, very much as he did at Horton, through those groves of Academe, generally to be found out of the crowd, in paths not much frequented, busy always, caring very little for pleasures by the way. As he got on, he became a little better known as having "coached" very effectually, but with little demonstration, several dunces for their smalls, and one or two better men for special subjects, especially theology: and so came through that part of his life with little fame, but such as it was, very good. Such a man leaves an impression, faint but lasting, and which is not dependent upon known and proved facts. This, indeed, is what almost everybody does one way or other. We don't know any harm that the good-for-nothing may have done, but we become aware by something in the air that he is a good-for-nothing; and we may have no act of virtue to set against a man's name, yet know that he is a good man by instinct, by an atmosphere about him, something like a moral taste of which we cannot explain the cause.

Mr. Asquith had this kind of reputation, if it can be called a reputation. He was poor; he had very little, if anything, more than the £100 a year which Mr. Prescott, the Rector, gave him. He was accustomed to spare living, and liked it, being unreasonably, and indeed wrongly, indifferent to what he ate and drank, and quite unworthy of the good cooking at the Rectory or the more pretentious efforts at the Hall. He liked his own chop at home quite as well, even when he had, as was sometimes necessary, to scrape off the cinders which it brought along with it from the gridiron, before he ate it. Mr. Asquith thought this was a very natural accident, and did not complain.

Such a man is the only man altogether independent in our complicated social system. He never remarked the ugly Kidderminster under his feet, or wished for a Persian rug in its

9

place. He did not mind in the least when his clerical coat got shabby. What did it matter? Everybody knew him on the one hand—nobody knew him on the other. In either case he was indifferent, and consequently independent. If there was anything he was a little particular over, it was his washing, his landlady said. The landlady was an old servant at the Rectory, who had been provided for in this curate's house, and who knew the ways of the kind. But she had never met with any like Mr. Asquith—no one who gave so little trouble, or was so easily satisfied.

But he was only the curate. Such qualities as his make little show. And after a while the Prescotts almost forgot that there was such a person in their neighbourhood. They said "How do you do, Mr. Asquith?" when they met him at the Rectory or on the road; but after they had done their duty by him, and asked him twice (which was really a superfluity of attention), he dropped into his own sphere, and save at Uncle Hugh's, or in church, by accident, was seen of them no more.

CHAPTER III

THE TWO TOGETHER

THE dinners at the Hall had not, however, been entirely without fruit in the lives of the two inconsiderable people who first met there. Mary, it may be supposed, had regarded with a little interest the appearance of the stranger, who was quite a new thing in her life. Few strangers came at Horton even when Percy was at home, and Percy had not been at home since Mary had finally developed into a young woman, and been permitted to wear a long frock and put up her hair; so that she had no acquaintance with new faces, and the appearance of an individual unknown, even though he was only the curate, aroused the liveliest interest and curiosity in her. He was not a handsome man, but he had the air of having a will and meaning of his own which is always attractive to a woman, even though he did not sing, nor play upon any instrument, nor know any games to speak of. These deficiencies did not affect Mary, who only played a little upon the piano, and though she was constantly called upon to make up her uncle's rubber, and had in consequence a very fair proficiency in whist, was not fond of games. Thus the remarks which were made upon Mr. Asquith afterwards were, Mary thought, so unjust so far beyond the measure of his delinquencies, even if he were a delinquent, that in her thoughts she immediately constituted herself his champion. In her thoughts, and a little in words too; she ventured to say: "I don't think he looks stupid at all," when Anna and Sophie, after the second entertainment to which he had been invited, broke forth simultaneously into the outcry, "Oh, what a stupid man!" The sound of this small voice, so unexpected, confounded the girls. They looked at her in amazement, and then they laughed.

"Why, here is a Daniel come to judgment," cried Sophie, and "Here is Mary setting up to have an opinion," said Anna. It was the most amusing thing that had happened for a long time.

"Well, why shouldn't Mary have an opinion?" said her uncle, "and about the curate, too, which is a subject young ladies are always supposed to understand."

"Mary must not trouble her head about curates," said Mrs. Prescott. "She is a great deal too young for any nonsense of that kind."

"Fancy calling Mr. Asquith nonsense!" cried both the girls

again, with a burst of laughter. They were not in the least interested, so that Mary's interference only amused them. If she had made herself the champion of a more eligible visitor, Sophie and Anna might not perhaps have taken it nearly so well.

"He doesn't look stupid, and there is no nonsense about him, and I think he is very nice," said Mary, but she was at that moment putting away her work, and spoke very low, almost to herself, and nobody paid any attention. She felt, however, a little excited at having thus, as it were, taken up her position and declared her sentiments. She felt like the champion of an injured but noble man—the defender of the unfortunate. This gives a sense of generosity, of fine elation to the mind. It seemed to Mary as if she were herself less insignificant in being thus the champion of another. And it gave her an interest in Mr. Asquith, which was entirely disinterested, but yet was akin, perhaps, to a sentiment more warm, of which as yet Mary had never thought even in her most romantic dreams.

And by-and-by it came to pass that these two met not unfrequently upon the roads, and sometimes in the cottages where Mary was often a visitor. She went there sometimes on charitable errands, and sometimes from mere kindness and liking for the good people, whom she had known all her life. The charity was not Mary's charity, it need hardly be said, for she had nothing of her own to give. Mrs. Prescott was not rich nor very interesting, nor a woman who talked much on any subject, especially upon that of the poor and their claims: but she had a kind heart. When there was a very nice pudding at luncheon, she almost always remembered that poor Sally Williams, who was in "a deep decline," and had no appetite, might be tempted by a bit of it, or if the chicken was very tender, she felt sure that old John Price, who had lost his teeth, or Mrs. Sims at the almshouses, would like it. "I will just put this nice little piece in a dish, and you will run down to the village with it, Mary," she would say, "as soon as you have finished, my dear."

"But why should Mary go?" some one remarked, at least three days out of five.

"She never has time to finish her luncheon," said Mr. Prescott, who loved a good meal.

"And why can't you send Pierce, mamma? I am sure she has always plenty of time for her dinner, and never hurries for any one."

"Oh, my dears," said kind Mrs. Prescott, "it tastes so much better when one of the young ladies takes it. Pierce would only go because she was obliged to go, and perhaps she would think it a bore, and fling it at them, so to speak."

"I darethay Mary findth it a bore, too," said John.

"Oh, never!" Mary would say. She was not one who cared to spend a great deal of time at table; and as soon as her aunt rose she was ready with her basket. She went so lightly skimming down the long shady avenue, like a bird or a fawn—but no—like nothing in the world, but a nice little happy-hearted, light-footed girl, conscious of going on an errand that would give pleasure, which is one of the sweetest, pleasantest, and fairest of sights to be seen in the world. She liked the errand dearly; she liked the little start of agreeable anticipation with which she was received (though her appearance could scarcely be said to be unexpected, it was so frequent), and the smile with which the invalid would greet her, and that delightful consciousness that it tasted sweeter from her kind little friendly hands than if Pierce had bounced in and thumped the basket down on the table, and taken no pains about it. Pierce did not always do this, but was kind, too, in her way. But nobody is quite just in their estimate of others, and this was what Mary thought.

And as often as not, Mr. Asquith would meet her on the way—sometimes as she was going, sometimes coming; sometimes in the cottages, sometimes as she came out smiling, with her empty basket. Of course Mr. Asquith gave all the credit of what was in reality Mrs. Prescott's kindness to her little niece. He thought this practical little girl, with her basket, acted on her own impulse, and that it was altogether out of the tenderness of her own heart that she remembered the little fancies of the sick. Most likely he thought that these little delicacies were saved from her own share of the good things at the Hall, and never made account of Mrs. Prescott at all in the matter; for nobody is quite just, as has been said, and Mrs. Prescott was stout and entirely uninteresting, and her under lip projected a little, so that people sometimes thought her cross and sometimes sulky. But Mary was as bright as the day, and the village people were all fond of her. "Oh, come in, sir," they said at first, when he lingered at the door, seeing a lady in the room. "I will come again another day, Mrs. Williams, for I see you have a visitor already." "Oh, bless you, sir, come in, come in; why it's only Miss Mary," the good woman would say, laughing with amused surprise at the thought that on such a consideration the curate should be shy and hold back.

And in this way many meetings came about without either of the two being aware that they were becoming used to seeing each

13

other, and that a little anticipation of this personal pleasure began to mingle with the kindness of their original motives.

When Mr. Asquith made the discovery that it was so, great discouragement fell upon his mind, such as had never moved it before. For nothing of the kind had ever before come in his hard-working way. What was Miss Mary to him, or Miss anything? He was a poor man, far too poor to marry. It had never occurred to him to think of his poverty before. Indeed, he was not poor, for he had few wants, and could always do very well with what he had; and he had never intended to marry, or thought of marrying. He might even, indeed—it was very likely, have said some things in his day about the iniquity of marrying when you have no means of supporting a wife, much less children, and when in all likelihood you are betraying some foolish girl who knows nothing of the world into lifelong penury, labour, and privation.

When he came to think of it, he felt sure that he had said many such things: and was it possible that he was so lost to every sense of duty, so forgetful of principle as to let himself fall into temptation in this way, and probably, possibly—a thought which made his grave face glow—lead another, another!—a young creature born to better fortune, almost a child—into the same snare? To describe the state of agitation into which the young man was brought by this sudden flash of perception is not easy—the sweetness of it, the misery of it, the keen, poignant, sharply-stinging delight. For though it was pain, it was delight, too. To be able to make her love him, that sweet little girl, Mary!

The world is hard, and it is bitter to give up, and to put a stop to that rising current of new life is enough to tax all a man's powers. But when you have said everything that can be said in that respect, there still remains the fact that the curate had, in one flash of consciousness, a moment of delight which nobody could take from him. He had tasted the sweetness, though the cup might not be for him; and then he fell headlong into the bitter depths below.

There must be no more of it, he said to himself, no more! And the first thing he did was to shut himself up, to take to his books, to give up his visiting; he would not even walk out for exercise save in the evening, when he was sure he could not meet her? Sacrifice her because he loved her? Oh no, never; such a thing could not be; but to sacrifice himself, that was not so hard; he thought he could do that. Therefore he departed from all his good ways as a parish priest, saying to himself that it was only for a time, and praying God to pardon that temporary neglect of duty because of the other more urgent duty which he must, he must carry out, at whatever cost that might be.

14

And Mary meantime had her own little thoughts, which nobody made much account of, and which at the present moment nobody suspected. But what those thoughts were wants a longer space than the end of this chapter to say.

CHAPTER IV

MARY'S LITTLE THOUGHTS

MARY'S mind was supposed to be very youthful and unformed. She had been kept longer a child than is usual, and yet, by reason of a sort of solitude in which she lived in the midst of a family which was, yet was not, absolutely her own family, her thoughts had exercised themselves silently on many subjects not commonly considered by children; but all in a shy and voiceless way, so that nobody round her had any conception of many reasonings which had gone on in her mind. When Mr. Asquith came to Horton she had been very curious about him, and when he failed to interest the rest, he became still more a curiosity and interest to Mary.

Among the subjects which occupied her silent thoughts there had been many little questions about the clergymen and their ways. As a matter of fact clergymen were more frequent visitors at Horton than any other class of men, and Mary had secretly been a critic of them all her life. Her Uncle Hugh was a clergyman whom she saw perpetually. He was a parish priest, with not very much to do, and one who was fully convinced that he did his duty. But Mary was not equally convinced. There was a good deal in his life which did not seem to that little critic to be much in harmony with what she read in her New Testament. To be sure, she knew well enough that every man who is in the Church can't go wandering about the world like St. Paul, teaching and preaching to the heathen.

Mary was aware that the change of times must be taken into account, and that the steady work of a parish has to be considered as well as the romance of missionary devotion. But she could not quite reconcile Uncle Hugh to the standard in which she believed, even after everything was taken into account. He was too comfortable, too much at his ease, had more spare time than he ought to have had, and, indeed, altogether was too like Uncle John, who was the merely secular head of the family, than satisfied the rigorous ideal of youth. There was indeed very little difference between Uncle Hugh and Uncle John. The elder brother sat in a little room which was called his business-room, whereas the special retirement of the other was spoken of as the study: and the parson wore a white tie instead of the cosy checked one which generally enveloped the throat of the Squire, and a black coat

16

instead of a shooting-jacket; but during the week these were the chief differences between them. Mary, all silent in the background, not considered by anybody to have an opinion at all, arraigned these two before her private tribunal, and was not satisfied, and concluded that there should have been a great deal more difference. To be sure, on Sunday there was difference enough. Uncle Hugh in his surplice was a commanding figure, and he preached while Uncle John yawned and listened. He was not a very good preacher.

None of these things are hid from the inexorable little judges from seven to seventeen, who give us all our due. In her heart, though she was fond of him, she was not satisfied with Uncle Hugh as a clergyman. His bishop was very well satisfied, but not Mary. And the curates were still less satisfactory. The High Church development was only in its beginning in those days, and curates made little or no pretensions to sacerdotal superiority, but were just young men in the Church, as their brothers were young men in the army. They were very good-natured young fellows most of them, very willing to give a shilling or even half-a-crown to poor old Hodge—not quite so willing to administer spiritual consolation or pray by his bedside—yet, by the aid of the service for the visitation of the sick, getting manfully through that too, and then, with a sigh of relief, coming up to croquet at the Hall. They had always time for croquet, and took enormously long walks, and had a considerable difficulty in getting through the long days in a dull little place where, as they would sometimes complain, there was nothing to do. Most of the young men who had been curates to Mr. Prescott of Horton Rectory, left him with the best of recommendations; but little Mary, that little Rhadamantha, had them all up at the bar before her, and judged them severely, though she never said a word.

But Mr. Asquith was something altogether new, and of a different order of being. When John said he was dull, and the girls that there was nothing in him, Mary demurred, as has been seen. She said to herself that Mr. Asquith was nice, and she liked the looks of him; and having thus, as it were, given herself from the first a brief in his defence, it was not so easy to put on the judge's cap and pronounce the verdict. Something, perhaps, from the beginning softened that judgment. She expected, to start with, that he would be different: and he was different. The dinners at the Hall bored him, which was a pity; and he would have none of the croquet, and instead of complaining that there was nothing to do, his excuse was that he had not time enough for the amusements which the young people of the parish set such store by. He had not

17

time. The other curates had not known what to do with their time. Certainly he was different.

And then Mary had begun to meet him about in all the cottages where there were sick people, where there was special need of kindness and help. He did not give away shillings, except rarely, for he had very few to give. He was not a young man on his promotion, waiting till the family living should be vacant, or till somebody should give him a benefice, but had thrown himself into his work as if he never meant to go away. Mary made some small investigations on this point in the most innocent and natural way. She said to the Rector, "Uncle Hugh, I suppose Mr. Asquith is going to stay longer than the other curates," at a moment when Mr. Prescott was unoccupied, and had time to answer the question.

"Eh?" cried the Rector, "Asquith stay longer? What makes you think so?"

"He talks as if he were always to be here," said Mary.

"Oh, do you think so? This little girl is not such a fool as she looks," said his reverence. "I've noticed that too."

"Don't speak to Mary so," said Mrs. Hugh Prescott, who was somewhat matter of fact. "She is not a fool at all, oh no; she has a great deal of observation. But Mr. Asquith had better not deceive himself, Hugh, for you know you have always liked a change of curates. Perhaps I had better say a word——"

The Rector's wife was fond of saying a word, which generally made the person addressed very angry, though she had no such meaning. Her husband stopped her with a movement of his hand. "Don't, my dear," he said. "It is not that he thinks too much of himself. He has not the prospects of the other young men. He is not serving his apprenticeship here with the hope of soon setting up for himself."

"You speak of the Church as if it were a trade, Hugh."

"Do I, my dear? Well, perhaps it is something the same after all, if you think of it—for most people are looking out for something better. I should not mind being a canon or a prebendary myself, or even a dean."

"And is not Mr. Asquith looking out for something better?" said Mary. She was more interested in this question than in any other that could at the moment be presented to her.

"Poor fellow! I don't know that he has anything better to look for," said the Rector. "He has few friends, and nobody to push him. I should not wonder if he remained a curate all his life."

"Nobody does that nowadays," said Mrs. Hugh Prescott. "Something always turns up. A poor clergyman, so far as I can see, has just as many chances as one that is well off. He is kind to somebody's child, or attends somebody's mother on her deathbed, or something of that sort. There is a special providence for poor curates, I think."

Mary took in all this with quick ears, and asked herself, whether, in reality, a special providence was all that Mr. Asquith had to look to. "There is none other that fighteth for us, but only Thou, O God," we say in church day by day: but even that pious sentiment seems to convey a veiled opinion that other aid would be desirable: but when it is said of a man that a special providence is wanted for his promotion, that man's hopes do not, to most of the world, seem particularly well founded. Mary felt with a curious swelling of her heart that she was glad this was the case with Mr. Asquith. She was proud of it, if pride is possible in such a matter. When she tested him by the first great commission which sent men out to preach without even bread in their scrip, much less money in their purse—that test which no one had borne as yet— she felt that at last here was one who could bear it; and this gave Mary a degree of pleasure quite incommensurate with his stay in the parish, or of any possible knowledge he could have of her, or she of him. After all she had nothing at all to do with it; and what were his principles of action, or how he was moved by the absence of all means of advancing himself, she had not the least way of knowing. It might be this that made him what John called dull. Mary could not tell. But she felt in her heart, though she was so ignorant, that the real clergyman for whom she had been looking had appeared at last—the only one who could bear the test which had not succeeded at all with the rest of the curates, nor even Uncle Hugh.

And this was the conclusion which had been formed in her mind even before she began to meet Mr. Asquith in the cottages. She was keenly alive to his demeanour there. It was as if she had gone to collect evidence upon this subject. When she was giving poor Sally Williams her pudding, she was at the same moment mentally weighing the curate and his manners to poor Mrs. Williams, and making him out. Perhaps Mary was not quite an impartial judge, being biassed, as has been said, by the other pieces of evidence which she had already put together, and even by something more subtle still, by her own foregone conclusion, and certain weakening prepossessions that had stolen into her heart. But about the time when Mr. Asquith took fright and began to shut himself up and relinquish his visits to the cottages, Mary had completed all her investigations, or had forgotten them, or had come to think them the most unnecessary, the most impertinent of inquiries, having somehow suddenly and unconsciously been led to the conclusion that there was nobody like Mr. Asquith, and that whatever he did became, from the fact of his doing it, right. It gave all the more weight to her opinion in this respect that she was not, as has been seen, a girl who naturally believed in curates, or took the excellence of that class for granted, as some young women do. It was, however, a somewhat severe test of Mary's faith that almost simultaneously with her full conviction of it, this perfect man should suddenly begin to conduct himself in so strange a way. For she could not help being struck by the fact that she met him no longer, even had the poor people been silent on the subject, which they were not. They poured out their complaints to her, sometimes quite simply, sometimes with a little mischievous meaning. "Mr. Asquith? We haven't seen Mr. Asquith, no—not for ten days; him as used to come in and give my poor Sally a comfor'able word 'most every day. I don't know what's the cause. I only hope, Miss Mary, as we've done nothing to offend him. It ain't with our will if we has, for a kinder gentleman never come inside my door."

"Oh, no, Mrs. Williams, I am sure he would not take offence. Perhaps he is very busy; you know a clergyman—has to study a great deal," said Mary, pausing to pick up the first excuse that came handy.

Mrs. Williams shook her head. "If it had been most clergymen," she said, "I shouldn't have wondered, for they soon tires—but Mr. Asquith! oh, he did seem another sort, he did!" the poor woman cried.

And then old Mrs. Sims at the almshouses had her little word to put in: "I can't think what's come over Mr. Asquith, that was such a kind gentleman. He's not come no more since the last time as he met you here, Miss Mary. It couldn't be as a fine, tall gentleman like 'im was afraid of you."

"Why should anyone be afraid of me?" Mary cried, with a laugh. But she was glad to get outside that keen-sighted old woman's cottage, for she felt the heat of a coming blush which swept all over her, up to the very roots of her hair, a blush which sent all her blood coursing through her veins, and made her feel disposed to laugh again, and then to cry. Afraid of her! Why should any one, much less the curate, be afraid of her, a little person who was only Mary, and whom nobody made any account of? But as she asked herself that question, Mary knew that it was so. She knew with a sudden flash of discovery, which was very wonderful and sweet, that Mr. Asquith was afraid of her, of loving her, and of betraying he loved her; and that he was making a stand against his heart and trying to avoid her, and put her out of his

20

life. It was a tremendous, overpowering discovery; but after she had got accustomed to the thought, Mary once more laughed in her heart; for she knew by instinct, though she had never had any experience, that these tactics were never successful, and that in this endeavour Mr. Asquith would fail.

CHAPTER V

SELF-BETRAYED

OF course Mary proved right. In such a small parish as Horton it was quite impossible that two people could live for many weeks without meeting each other. The curate might shut himself up for a few days. He might say he was busy with his sermon; he might say he had a headache; he might acknowledge that his activity in the parish and all the institutions he had set up had thrown him into arrears with his reading, and such intellectual work as is necessary for a man who has to write two sermons every week. But this could not last for ever. Mary, who was so simple and so sweet, was not like those powers of darkness whom we must resist till they flee from us; indeed, Mary was so far different that when she was resisted she did not flee. She was so clever that she divined at once that in resisting the charm of her mild society poor Mr. Asquith had made a confession of his weakness, and it gave her a great and, it is to be feared, a mischievous amusement to watch how long he would keep to that. Alas! he could not keep to it very long. He was obliged to go to the rectory to communicate with his chief, and he could not help meeting Mary there. He had even to walk with her as far as the lodge, to carry something that was too heavy for her, and then Mary behaved very badly to the poor curate. She put on an air of sympathy to conceal her amusement, and she said, "I am afraid you have not been well lately, Mr. Asquith. I have not seen you anywhere about."

"No," said the curate, with his heart sinking, "I have been—not very well."

"I am so sorry," said the little hypocrite. "I hope you don't find that Horton does not suit you: and just when you have got so well into the work."

"Oh, it is not that it doesn't suit me," the curate said, "quite the reverse. The air is very pure and sweet." He gave a side glance at her as he spoke, and it is to be feared that it was Mary and not the air he was thinking of when he used these words.

"Poor Sally Williams is longing to see you," said Mary. "I go often, but I am not the same good. She likes her pudding, but I can't talk to her as you do, Mr. Asquith; and they say," continued the girl, with a soft shade of awe coming over her face, "that she has not very long to live."

"You teach me my duty," cried the curate, quite

overwhelmed. "I have been very neglectful. I shall certainly not miss another day."

"And old Mrs. Sims thinks you have forgotten the old people at the almshouses. She shakes her head and says, 'Ah, I never thought as he'd keep it up like that: they never does,' Mrs. Sims says."

"Thank you so much for telling me," said Mr. Asquith; "indeed it was not inadvertence. I knew that I was neglecting one duty: but I thought, perhaps, it might be excusable on account of another."

"Oh, Mr. Asquith!" cried Mary, "I never meant to say you neglected anything, you must not think so. But ought a person to neglect one duty on account of another? You said the other day in your sermon——"

"Oh! don't talk to me about my sermon. It was a poor performance off the book, when I had no experience; but you are right, we have no warrant to forget one duty for the sake of another. The part of a true man is to do all, and not to flinch. The spirit is willing, but oh! the flesh is very weak."

I hope the reader will not think badly of Mary if I allow that the agitation of the curate filled her with a sort of elation and mischievous triumph for the moment. She had nearly laughed in the face of his gravity, and if she had done what was in her heart she would have cried out, "All this bother about a little girl like me!" But she did not say anything; she did not laugh; and when she looked up into his face for a moment at the lodge-gate, when he gave the books he was carrying for her to Mrs. Martingale, the coachman's wife, to be sent up to the house, Mary was filled with sudden compunctions, and felt disposed rather to cry. She waved her hand to him as she went up the avenue with an April sort of face, half smiling, half weeping, which gave him a great deal of thought as he turned sadly upon his own way. He did not know what it meant, poor young man! It looked as if she were sorry for him, but why should she be sorry for him? Did she see, did she understand, the cause of his trouble? did she mean to support him with her sympathy, or to mock him, or to show him how far, far he was out of her sphere? He thought a great deal more about this than was at all consistent with the many other things he had to think of, and, alas! got the books of the lending library entirely into disorder, and forgot how much money he had received that week from the penny-bank and the clothing-club. He put down twice as much as they had paid to each subscriber's name, and had to make it up from his own poor little purse; fortunately the entire amount was not considerable, but it was a great deal too much to be taken out of his poor pocket by Mary's little regretful, sympathetic, yet mischievous look.

To tell the truth, Mary's heart was bounding along the avenue like a bird, though her feet went soberly enough. It was so light, there was no keeping it still; it sang little trills of pleasure along the way, and mounted up towards heaven, and found a new brightness over all the earth. To think that she who was only Mary should suddenly have become the princess of a kingdom all her own—to think that she should be all at once of consequence enough to make a man abandon all his duties! It was indeed very wrong of a man in Mr. Asquith's position to abandon any of his duties for the sake of this little girl: but Mary did not see it in that light. As she walked by herself up the avenue she laughed loud out, and then felt dreadfully ashamed of herself, and dried her eyes, which were full of tears. How foolish it was of him! To say even to herself that this man, who was the best man she had ever met, was foolish, was a sort of delightful little sin to Mary, a piece of profanity—a small wickedness. How dared she say he was foolish? and yet—oh! how foolish he was. How nice of him to be so silly! Perhaps he was afraid that she did not care for him, would not have him if he asked her? No doubt that was what he was afraid of. To think that he knew Latin and Greek and theology, and all manner of things, and could read German, yet could not read what was in Mary's eyes! She sat down by the roadside, before the house was in sight, not daring to see anybody, glad to be alone, to have time to think over again what he said and how he looked, and to say to herself how silly it was!

All this time, as will be seen, Mary had not the faintest enlightenment as to what it was that Mr. Asquith feared. She never thought of his poverty, of what it is to be a poor curate or a poor curate's wife, without hope of advancement, or money enough to keep the wolf from the door. She thought only of him, and how glad she would be to do everything for him—to live in a cottage, and look after her own little housekeeping, and make him comfortable, more comfortable than ever he had been in his life, and to help him and work with him. She thought that to be the first in all the world to one who was the first in all the world to her, was the fairest fate that earth could give. She had no doubt on the subject, or fear—for how could she tell, who had never had above a few shillings in her life, how much two people require to live upon? or how could she take into consideration other consequences, which were more serious still?

Mr. Asquith went to see Sally Williams that day, and for many days after, as long as the poor girl lived, but never again did

24

he meet Mary there. He did not see her at the almshouses, he encountered her nowhere—which indeed was a little instinctive coquetry mingled with modesty on Mary's part: for she would not, after having exerted herself to bring him back, allow him to find her in his way, as if that had been what she wanted. And now it was the curate's turn to be astonished, and to feel himself injured. Though he had retired from his daily duties in order to avoid Mary, he felt himself sadly aggrieved, now that he had returned to them, to find that Mary avoided him. Instead of congratulating himself that they were both of accord, and that in this way his purpose would be the better accomplished, this inconsistent young man felt sadly disappointed, taken in, cheated, and ill-used. Why had she spoken to him so, if she had meant to conclude their intercourse in this way? Mr. Asquith's annoyance was all the greater from the fact that Mary did not neglect her little offices of charity in order to avoid him as he had done in order to avoid her. She was cleverer than he was, so far as this went, and had her faculties more free. He was always hearing wherever he went that Miss Mary had just gone. "It is not five minutes since Miss Mary went. She is that good," said poor Mrs. Williams, "now that my poor girl is sinking, she never misses a day." "You're kindly welcome, Mr. Asquith, sir," said the old woman at the almshouse. "Take that chair, sir. It's one as was set for Miss Mary. She was scarce gone when I see you coming." Mr. Asquith was fretted beyond description by these perpetual missings. He could not get them or her out of his head. Sometimes he was more angry than words can say. He thought she did it on purpose (which was not far from the truth), in order to show him how presumptuous he was, and how impossible that she could ever care for him (which was not the truth at all). And at last the poor curate was wrought to such a point of exasperation that he made up his mind, when he did meet her, that he would tell her what she had done, and how cruelly she had treated him, and then leave the parish altogether. But he would not go without letting her know. She should be made aware that what was sport to her was death to him. To have wrung a man's heart and spoiled his life might appear to her a small matter, but the curate was resolved that so far he would have his revenge, since he could have nothing else, and that she should know what she had done.

They met at last quite accidentally, in the quietest road, where their interview was certain not to be disturbed by any intruder. At least, it can scarcely be said that they met; he was jogging wearily, determinedly along, thinking how he never saw her, and how he must see her, once at least, before the end of all things, when suddenly the grey frock he knew so well appeared round the corner of a cross road, and Mary, not seeing him, went on before him, tranquilly, on her way home. The curate's heart stood still. Should he, now that the matter was in his own hands, put off the crisis? Should he have it out now once for all? After standing still for that one moment, his heart bounded up into his throat, wildly beating, and in a long stride or two Mr. Asquith was at Mary's side.

And now for the vials of wrath that were to be poured out, the passion of love and reproach that was to end all their intercourse, and with it that glimpse of a sweeter life which had come suddenly to the curate in Horton! But when he came up with her he was breathless, partly from haste, partly from agitation, and it was Mary who said the first word. She looked up into his face surprised and smiling, with a sweetness that went to his very heart. There was no guilty consciousness in her eyes. She did not look at him as one who had sinned against him, as one who felt that he had something to reproach her with, but with a look of pleasure, as if she were quite happy in this unexpected meeting. "Oh, Mr. Asquith, is it you? What a long time it is since I have seen you!" she said, in her pleasant voice.

"It is a long time," said the curate, panting: and then he added, "I fear I have made you change your hours and your habits, which is more than I am worth."

"Change my hours and my——. I haven't got any hours or habits," cried Mary, "and indeed I don't know what you mean."

"Oh, Miss Mary!" he cried. I don't think he knew her surname at all, or if he once knew it he had forgotten it, for Mary was the only name he ever heard given to her. "Oh, Miss Mary!" he cried, "I never meet you now in any of the cottages wherever I go: and I know how that is. I know that you have seen what was going on in my presumptuous mind: but there was no presumption in it, if you only knew. I know very well I am poor—as poor as—as poor as a church mouse, as people say,—too poor to ask any woman to share my miserable fortunes. Don't, don't for heaven's sake be afraid of me! If I can't help thinking of you, at least I can help saying it. I gave up my visiting when I saw what was coming: but you spoke to me yourself on that subject. You said, had a man a right to neglect his duty for the sake of—for the sake of—— And I knew that what you said was just. From that day I made up my mind to go on with all my usual visiting, and to go on seeing you, which was always sweet though cruel; to go on as if it did not matter, only never to say a word——"

26

"And what has made you change your resolution, Mr. Asquith?" said Mary, very demurely, without raising her eyes.

"Change? I have not changed at all," he said. And then he stopped short, with a look of misery and confusion. "What have I done?" he said. "What have I done? though I did not intend it—it has been too much for me—I have betrayed myself after all!"

And for a moment he turned his back upon her, as if he would have fled.

"Don't run away," said Mary, softly touching his arm with her hand. "Why shouldn't you tell me—whatever you wanted to tell me?—if you did really want to tell me anything," she said.

"Oh, Mary!" cried the curate, and paused; for the words came so fast upon him that he did not know which to say first.

"Yes?" said Mary softly, giving him one little sidelong glance: and then her face crimsoned over, and she drooped her head, but still with a modest note of interrogation in the turn of her fine little pink ear.

CHAPTER VI

PARADISE LANE

"WE must tell them all directly," Mary said.

"Tell them!" cried the curate. For one brief half hour he had forgotten everything, and given himself up to that delight which once in his life every man has a right to—or so at least we think when we are young—the delight of loving and being loved. The bare country road had turned into Paradise, into Elysium for both of them; it was more beautiful and sweet than anything out of heaven. The green boughs waved softly between them and the celestial blue above, making a chequer-work of sun and shade that flickered and danced, and made the very dust under their feet happy; and as for the flowers in the hedgerows, no roses were ever so sweet. They walked upon enchanted ground, and all nature sang soft hymns of praise over their happiness, which was sweeter than the roses, or anything that earth, our homely foster-mother, can give. She was wistfully glad of it, that brown and faithful nurse, that mother earth, who could strew flowers at their feet, but could not bestow such blessedness. But when Mary said those simple words, the world, which had nothing to do with that hour, suddenly rolled its great shadow round, coming between the curate and the sunshine of heaven. "Tell them!" he said, and his countenance fell. Oh yes, he knew very well they must be told: but he had been able to forget it for that moment of delight.

"Yes, tell them. You meant that?" said Mary, looking up somewhat alarmed in his face.

"Oh yes, I meant that," he said with a groan—"at least, I didn't mean anything. I never meant to tell you, let alone them."

"So you said," Mary remarked, in her demure way; "you told me you had made up your mind not to tell me——" and she laughed in the pleasure of her maiden power.

"Oh, my darling!" the curate said, "it would have been better if I had not told you. It would have been better if I had gone away, and smothered my heart or myself, if necessary, rather than have brought this trouble on you."

"Trouble!" she cried, and laughed. Mary was not a bit afraid. She was as ignorant as the bird who was singing little saucy songs and melodious gibes at them overhead, calling on all his bird neighbours to make fun of the lovers, who had waited for June and full summer, instead of building their nests like prudent folk in the early spring. Mary knew about as much as the thrush did on the subject of ways and means—and she was not afraid.

"They will not hear me speak," he said; "they will ask me how I could dare to think of dragging you down into my poverty? I know that is what they will do—and they will be right," he added with a great sigh.

Mary paused a little in surprise, and then she asked, "I wonder what you think I am? Do you think I am rich?"

"No," he said, pressing her hand close to his side. "Thank heaven! I know you are not rich."

"I see very little to thank heaven about," said Mary, "on that score: perhaps you think that I have great prospects, or that somebody is going to leave me a great deal of money, or—something. Why, I have not a penny in the world! And my aunt is always shaking her head and saying, 'If anything happens to your uncle!' Do you know what I should have to do then? I should have to go out as a governess, if anybody would have me to teach their children—or perhaps as a maid in the nursery."

"Oh, hush!" he cried. "You a maid in the nursery! But, Mary darling, you would be almost better as a governess than you will be with me. Do you know how much I have a year? A hundred pounds and my lodging, and I don't know where I am to get any more."

"A hundred pounds! I never had a hundred shillings of my own. It seems quite a great sum," said Mary. "I should think we could do very well upon that. We must have a cottage of our own though. I have often thought a cottage might be made very pretty if one were to take a little trouble. I should like it so much better than a big house."

"Oh, Mary, you little angel! You have just come astray out of heaven, and you know nothing about this hard world," he cried.

"Oh, don't I?" said Mary, with a laugh of superior wisdom,—"much more than you do, I am sure, though you are so much cleverer than I. We could not have many servants, that's true. But what is the good of them—except to get in each other's way, and make aunt cross? I'll tell you what I shall have. I'll have a nice strong big girl out of the schools, and train her myself: and you'll see, after a while, all the ladies will be contending to get one of the girls whom Mrs. ——"

Here Mary paused, and blushed redder than ever, and with a cough turned her head away.

"Finish your sentence," said the happy curate, too happy for the moment to remember how foolish it was. "Mrs. ——? Finish what you were going to say."

"You know well enough," said Mary, who in the delightful fervour of settling everything had thus been carried away so much farther than she intended. She added after a moment in a lower tone, "You know it is a very funny name."

"I think now it is the sweetest name in the world. Mary Asquith," he said—"Mrs. Asquith—I prefer it to any in the world."

"Well," said Mary, considering, "it has this for it, that it is not just like anybody's name. It has a great deal of character in it. You don't forget it as soon as you have heard it, like Smith or Brown."

"It is an old name," he said, with a little pride, "and one very well known in Cumberland, and known only for good, Mary. But," he added suddenly, after this outburst, "you are not to suppose that I am claiming to belong to a great family. Oh no, we are only yeomen; we are not equal to the Prescotts. We have an old house, which will be my brother's, but not like Horton—a homely old place, no better than a farmhouse. That is another thing that will be against me," he said, his voice sinking out of its happiness and pride into subdued tones.

"There cannot be anything against you," said Mary, giving a little pressure to his arm. "Do you think I am such a prize? They will be glad, I shouldn't wonder, to get me off their hands; my poor aunt will not have to say any more, 'Mary, if anything happens to your uncle!' I shall have my own—person," she said, pausing for a word, and laughing over it, "my own—person to take care of me— and what more does any girl require?"

Mr. Asquith was cheered, and yet not quite cheered, by these encouragements. He was very happy, and yet quite miserable. Nothing could take away from him the delight and glory which had fallen upon him out of heaven in that homely green lane of Paradise. But—his mind made a leap forward, or backward rather, to the things he had seen, to the facts of life which he knew, to the hard, hard existence of poverty. Had any man a right to drag down a woman, a girl so gently bred as Mary, into that gulf? had any man a right to bring children into the world with no bread to give them? He had held very distinct views upon this subject, and had sworn to himself that he never would so sin against the innocent, against the unborn. How often had he seen what followed in other poor clerical houses! He had seen the pretty young bride, all unthinking, all unfearing, pleased with her little house, and her married dignity, dragged down into a careworn troubled woman, a hard-working woman, with rough hands and a burdened mind, manual labour, and mental care, her strength and her heart both failing as the heavy years went on. To think of Mary, so young and

30

sweet, so thoughtless and lighthearted, so ignorant, bless her! of all these horrible realities, sinking, sinking year by year into such a woman—and by his means! The curate shrank within himself, his heart seemed to contract with a great pang. By his means! all because he could not contain himself, could not keep silent; could not love her without betraying his love. Oh, what a thing it was, that highest of human sentiments, that it could not curb a man's tongue, or restrain his impulses! That a man should love and yet not be able to keep silent, to spare the object of his love! He might have loved her all his life, and his love would have been a sweetness and a strength to him; but he ought to have respected her innocence and her youth, and never have told it, locked it up in his own bosom. If he had never spoken, God bless her! that would have given her a pang: but had he gone away, in a little time she would have forgotten him. But now, there could be no forgetting— now there was no going back—and she herself would insist upon the consummation of this sacrifice, upon giving him the solace of her sweet companionship, making him happy, making herself a servant, enduring toil, and privation, and care for his sake. For the curate knew that, whatever any one might say, it was the woman that had the worst of it. He would have to submit that she should be his servant, executing even menial offices, with those hands which he might kiss and reverence, but whose work he could not do. The woman had the worst of it: and he knew so many cases,— some where she had sunk altogether into a half cook, half nurse—a careworn creature spoiled with toil; and some in which she had developed into a patient angel, sacred and consecrated in her labours and sufferings. Mary would be that, the lover thought; and yet, who could tell that she would be that? and who could dare to open to a woman's feet that path of tears and bid her tread it, whatever might await her at the end? He went home to his lodgings with his heart bleeding, although his brain was giddy with happiness, and with the desire to believe that in his case there might be a difference, and that, for once, for once, all precedents notwithstanding, things might go well.

As for Mary, there never was a lighter heart than that with which she ran up the avenue, in too great a flutter and ferment to walk steadily, too happy to keep still. She felt as if she had wings, as if she trod upon air, and burst out singing, as she ran along under the trees, from pure joy. She had got her little promotion, the only promotion of which her life was capable. She had got her own world, her own life, her own share of the universe of God. To be sure she had been happy enough all her life, but how colourless that life looked amid the light and sunshine that streamed upon

31

this! "Only Mary" in a house full of people was more important, and Mrs. Asquith in her own house, the dispenser of happiness, the little monarch of all she surveyed! What a difference! What a difference! These were the secondary matters, the first beyond all comparison being him, the man out of all the world whom God had chosen for Mary. It seemed to her that a whole long chain of special providences had brought them together. That he should have come here, of all places in the world—he for whom every parish in England would have competed had they but known. That he should have come to the Hall, and yet not fallen in with the ways of the Hall, or fallen in love with Anna or Sophie, which would have been so much more likely. That he should have met her, and liked her, Mary, the little one who was of no account, best! Could such things have happened had not the heavens specially interested themselves, and taken unusual trouble to bring it all about? Even the meeting this morning was providential, for she was to have gone off on a visit the very next day, and in the meantime a hundred things might have happened to close his mouth. And to think that he should have been so frightened to speak. Oh, how foolish men were sometimes, though they were also so clever! What great prospects did he suppose she could have to make him not good enough for her? Not good enough for her! It was almost with a little shriek of happiness, and scorn, and admiration that Mary commented to herself upon his intentions and his self-reproaches. The foolish fellow! the darling! the noble, humble, good!—everybody but himself knowing how much too good for her he was.

Women have a great deal to bear in this world. Their lot is in many respects harder than that of men, and neither higher education, nor the suffrage, nor anything else can mend it. But there is one moment at least in which a girl has always the best of it, and that is when she has just accepted her lover. At that blissful epoch she has all the pleasure, with little or nothing of the care. It is he who has to encounter the anxious father or careful trustee. He has to meet the scoff with which those personages receive the trembling announcement of a small, a very small income. He has to think where the money is to come from to set up the new household. She has the best of it for once in her life. Afterwards the tables are turned. Not always, perhaps, but very often; and always, I am inclined to think, when poverty is the lot.

But Mary thought of none of all these things; with her it was all sunshine. She could scarcely keep from bursting out with her great news to everyone she met. To sit down at lunch and eat as if nothing had happened was almost an impossibility. If they only knew! They might have known, indeed, had they looked at her, that something had happened. But nobody took any notice. A slight accident had happened to John, of which he was discoursing at great length. "I thlipped," he said, "on the grass; there was nothing to make me thlip that I could see. It was thlippery with the rain, or because Morton had mowed it this morning. It was the strangest thing I ever thaw. On the grass—the thimplest thing! But I might have thprained my ankle. Yes, I might. I can't think how I didn't thprain my ankle," said John.

"But you didn't, you see, so it doesn't matter," said his father.

"He might have, though; and what a thing that would have been!" Mrs. Prescott remarked, who was more sympathetic, and had a great leaning to her eldest son.

"Yes, it would have been a very bad busineth," said John.

And that was the sort of talk that was going on while Mary sat beaming, and nobody found her little secret out.

CHAPTER VII

THE DISCLOSURE

MR. PRESCOTT spread himself out before the fireplace, standing with his legs apart, and his coat tails extended. There was, of course, no fire in the month of June, but an Englishman spreading himself out upon his own hearthrug, like a cock on his appropriate elevation, is more an Englishman than at any other moment. The Squire looked benevolently, yet severely upon the curate, who sat before him, twisting his soft hat in his hands. This was the only sign of embarrassment Mr. Asquith showed, but it was very discernible. He sat with his face turned towards his judge, without any shrinking or quailing, a little pale, very self-possessed and quiet. It was a very serious moment, and that the curate well knew.

"My niece!" Mr. Prescott said, and his countenance cleared a little, for he had thought at first that it must be one of the princesses of his house that this man was wooing. "Mary! why, Mary is not old enough for this sort of thing. How old is she? Why, she is only a child!"

"You have got used to considering her a child, Mr. Prescott; but I believe she is one-and-twenty, if you will inquire."

Mr. Prescott made a calculation within himself, and after a moment said, "So she is: I believe she is in her two-and-twentieth year. Who would have thought it! You must know," he added, "Mr. Asquith—though I don't know what your ideas may be on that subject—that though Mary is my niece, she has no money, not a penny. My sister was sadly imprudent in her marriage. Her orphan child, of course, had a home with me, but there is nothing in the way of fortune, not a sou."

"So I understood," said the curate, "otherwise I should never have ventured to approach her, being myself so poor a man."

"Ah!" said the Squire, looking at him doubtfully; then he added with cheerfulness, "You are still on the first step, Mr. Asquith, there is no telling how far you may go."

"I am not the stuff of which bishops are made," said the curate, with a short laugh.

"Well, there is no telling," said the other; and then he entered upon business. "You will understand," he said, "that I must make certain inquiries before going any farther. In the

34

matter of family now. We are not rich people, but in that respect we Prescotts have certain pretensions——"

"In that respect it is very easy to answer you, Mr. Prescott. So far as old family goes, mine is old enough. We have been in Cumberland in direct descent, father and son, settled in the same place, for three hundred years. But——" Mr. Prescott had been nodding his head in approval, saying to himself that he knew Asquith was a good name in the North. He looked up, but only with the faintest shadow on his face, at the curate's "but."

"But," repeated Mr. Asquith firmly, "though we are an old-established race, we are not what you would call gentry, Mr. Prescott. My father is of the old class of statesmen in Cumberland——"

"What is that?" asked the Squire hastily.

"It is, I suppose, what you call yeomen in the South."

"Oh!" said Mr. Prescott. He recovered from this shock, however, in shorter time than might have been expected; for a substantial yeoman is a very respectable personage, and there are often nice little hoards of money behind them; and then it was only Mary, after all.

"I don't pretend to say that I should not have been better pleased had you sprung from a family of gentry, Mr. Asquith; but after all, to have a family of any kind is something in these days. And you, of course, have had the education of a gentleman." The curate winced a little at this, not liking the idea that he had not always been a gentleman, even though he had the moment before disowned any such pretensions. But he did not betray his impatience, and Mr. Prescott continued, "The most important point is: you propose to marry my niece: what have you to support her? I have told you she has nothing of her own. Are you in circumstances to keep her in the position to which she has been accustomed? Your private means——"

"Mr. Prescott," said the curate crushing his hat in his tremulous hands, "that is exactly the question—that is the painful part—I have nothing. I have no private means; I have no expectations to speak of. My father, when he dies, will leave me perhaps some trifle—a few hundred pounds; but the fact is, I have nothing—nothing but my income from my curacy." He had not strength enough to meet the Squire's astonished gaze. His head drooped forward a little. "I am aware that you must think me presumptuous to the last degree, even careless of her comfort—for I have nothing but my poverty to offer—nothing——" for once in his life Mr. Asquith's courage fairly failed him, and he would have liked to run away, and be heard of in Horton no more. Oh, happy Mary, before whom no such ordeal lay!

"This is a very strange statement, Mr. Asquith," the Squire said.

The curate assented with a movement of his head; he could not say any more.

"It is a very strange statement," Mr. Prescott repeated. "You don't expect, I hope, that I—with the many calls upon me——"

Mr. Asquith half got up from his chair; he raised his hand, half deprecating, half indignant.

"I have a great many claims upon me," said the Squire reassured; "the estate does not bring in half it once did. You know as well as I do how landed property has deteriorated; and my second son is in the army, and has a great many expenses, and my girls to be provided for—I cannot be responsible for anything so far as Mary is concerned. I have given her her education and all that, but as for any allowance——"

"If she had anything of the sort, do you think I could ever have spoken?" the curate said.

Mr. Prescott was reassured: there was obvious sincerity in this disclaimer. He stood for a moment silent with a perturbed countenance, and then he said suddenly, "That's all very well, Mr. Asquith, but you're not like a silly girl who knows nothing—you've some acquaintance with the world. It is quite right of you to express such sentiments. But if you marry her, how are you to keep her? that is the question for me."

"Sir," said the curate, "you have a right to say anything—everything on that subject. It is the question, I know all the gravity of it. It is what I cannot answer even to myself."

"If you would not have spoken in the other case, supposing she had something of her own—how was it that you spoke now?" said the Squire, pushing his advantage; "a man ought to be able to deny himself in such circumstances. Men of your cloth permit themselves freedoms which other poor men don't. A parson marries and has a large family, and everybody is sorry for him, whereas, if it was a poor soldier who did it, or a clerk in a public office, or——"

The curate did not speak, it was all perfectly true. He had said the same himself a hundred times. He had said, even to the unfortunate culprit himself, that a clergyman, because he was a clergyman, had no right. And now it was brought home to himself, and he had not a word to say.

"What does my brother Hugh give you?" said the inexorable Squire. "A hundred a year? I suppose it is as much as he can

36

afford. And how are you to live with a wife on a hundred a year? How do you live on it without a wife? Percy, besides his pay, costs me—but that is nothing to the purpose. I ask you, can you live on it yourself, Asquith, without any supplement, without anything from home?"

The curate smiled somewhat grimly. Anything from home! He had been obliged to pay back to his poor father various sums expended on his education, which was a very different thing from receiving help from home. He said, "I have been able to manage—without any assistance," in a subdued tone. It was not pleasant to be thus cross-examined, but the Squire had a right to ask all manner of questions. He had put himself in Mr. Prescott's power.

"Supposing you have—I think it's very much to your credit. And there's the lodgings, of course, that's always something. But supposing you have—how are you to keep a wife? And have you thought of the consequences, sir?" said the Squire severely. "If it was only a wife even; but you know what always follows—half-a-dozen children before you know where you are. How are you to educate them, sir? How are you to feed them? How are you to set them out in the world? And yet you come and ask me, a man that has seen such things happen a hundred times, to give you my niece."

Mr. Asquith blushed like a girl at this suggestion. Mary herself was scarcely more modest, more delicate in all such embarrassing questions. And though he was not a humorous man by nature, a gleam of the ludicrous made its way into the question through the fierce countenance of the Squire. "These consequences," he said, "cannot come all at once. They will take a few years at least: and I don't calculate on staying always at Horton. In a town, in a large parish, curates have better pay."

"And are worked off their feet, they and all their belongings, their wives made drudges of, regular parish women, Bible women, or whatever you call them. I know what goes on in large parishes, in great towns. And the children grow up on the streets. No, the country's bad enough, but at least they can get fresh air and milk in the country, and people may be kind to them: and there's always a schoolmaster or someone to give them a little education."

"Mr. Prescott," said the curate mildly, "the children you are so kindly anxious about are not born yet, and perhaps never will be. Don't let us go any farther than is necessary. The question in the meantime concerns only Mary and myself."

"And how long will that be the case?" cried the Squire. But presently he calmed down. "You might get food perhaps," he said. "I say perhaps—I don't see how you are to do it—but allow that you could get food out of it, and a cottage to live in—where are your clothes to come from? Where are your shoes to come from? Mary is a lady; she has been brought up to have servants to wait upon her. Is my niece to be your housemaid, Mr. Asquith? your cook, and your washerwoman, and everything? You should marry somebody that is used to that sort of thing. Somebody who has the strength for it. Somebody in your own class of life!"

The curate rose up with a flush of anger on his face. He could keep his temper, but yet it stung him, all the more that it was just enough, and he had already said all this to himself. He said, "I fear it will do no good to talk of it longer, Mr. Prescott—you drive me to despair. And I don't deny that it is all true, everything you say. But I shall not always be curate at Horton. I shall not always continue a curate even, I hope. Sometimes, even without much influence, if a man does his work well, promotion comes."

"Very seldom," said the Squire.

"Still it comes sometimes: and if ever man had an inducement to work—will you think it over and try to look upon it more favourably? I know what a sacrifice it must be for her. Still, she has a right to choose too."

"To choose—at her age—knowing nothing of the world! Whatever you felt, sir, you should have kept it to yourself—you should not have spoken. How is a girl to know?"

"I thought so too," said the poor curate, humbly. "But a man has not always command of himself."

"A man ought always to have command of himself when another person's comfort is concerned, especially a clergyman, who makes more profession of virtue than other men," said the Squire, following him to the door, and sending that last volley after him. Mr. Asquith went away from the Hall a miserable man. He had not the heart to ask for Mary, to tell her how he had failed. As he hurried away, however, down the avenue, his heart, which had sunk altogether, began to rise a little in indignation. Why a clergyman more than other men? That a clergyman should be shut out from that side of life altogether was comprehensible. He might take vows as in the Church of Rome, there was reason in that. When men were so poor as he was, instead of tantalising them with the idea of freedom, and exposing them to all its risks, it might be better if they were under the protection of vows and forbidden to marry. But as that was not so, and the English ideal was quite different, why should it be worse in a clergyman than in other men? A clergyman could not struggle and push for promotion. He could not compete and shoulder his way through the crowd. Must he give up also all that made existence sweet?

38

And then the further question arose, would it have been better for Mary had he held his tongue and gone away and never told her he loved her? Had he perhaps closed that chapter to her too? Perhaps she might have forgotten him, and learned to love a richer man. But then perhaps she might not. Naturally a man feels that a woman who has learned to love him will not easily change, or transfer her affections to another. Would it not have been a wrong to Mary had he kept silence, had he never told her? It is better even to love and lose, the poet says, than never to love at all. It is better to have the triumph and delight of knowing that you are loved, even if that love never comes to any earthly close. Why should Mary have lost that because they were both poor? Nobody could take away from them that moment of blessedness, that sense of sweetest union, even if they might never marry at all—never—

But here a pang which was very acute and poignant like a sword went through the curate's heart. Never marry at all! Lose her, leave her, be parted from her, after what they had said to each other! Oh, what deep shadows come along with the brightest sunshine of life! What was the good of living at all, of having known each other, of having recognized the loveliness and sweetness of existence, if this was what had to be?

39

CHAPTER VIII

NEVERTHELESS

THE reader who is experienced, and knows how things go in this world, especially in questions of love and marriage, will not be surprised to hear that notwithstanding this troublous passage and several more, Mary was married to the curate in the autumn of that same year. When two people have set their hearts on this conclusion, it is astonishing how very seldom they are foiled, or disappointed in it. One or the other must break down in resolution: there must be a faint heart somewhere before parents or guardians or trustees or any authorities whatsoever can resist them. In the present case the authorities were weaker than usual, for they were not agreed. Mr. Prescott, to his astonishment, found that even his wife was not at one with him on this important question. He hurried to the morning room in which she was sitting to tell her, still in all the excitement of the discussion with the curate; but his fervour was chilled by the very first words she said. "I let him know very clearly what my opinion was. I told him that this sort of thing was doubly culpable in a clergyman. Between ourselves, it is only clergymen who do it. They believe in some sort of miracle, I suppose—feeding by the ravens, or that sort of thing: or else they expect to be maintained by the girl's family; but I soon let him see that nothing of the kind was to be looked for here."

"I hope, however, you didn't send him away for good, John?" said Mrs. Prescott, with a serious look.

"Send him away for good! I daresay he did not see much good in it: but I gave him a very decided answer, if that is what you mean."

"Well," said Mrs. Prescott, "I don't mean to say that it would be a good marriage for Mary: but very few men come to Horton at all, and we can't expect to live for ever, and it would be better that she should have somebody to take care of her. I am not a matchmaker, you know. I have been so too little, for there are Sophie and Anna still. But I do think that in certain circumstances you ought to be very careful how you reject an offer. If anything were to happen to us, what would become of your niece? The girls might not care to have her always with them, and it would not be at all suitable to have her here with John. She would be in a very embarrassing position, poor child—one trying for all of them. But if she had a husband to take care of her——"

40

"A husband who could not give her bread, much less butter to her bread."

"Oh, no one can ever tell. Someone with a living to give away might take a fancy to him: clergymen have many ways of ingratiating themselves. Or he might get a curacy in a town, where the pay is better, and where it is important to get a man who can preach. He is a very good preacher, far better than your brother Hugh, who always sends me to sleep. I don't know why you should reject Mr. Asquith. He has a great many things in his favour, and Mary likes him. Has she told me? Well, without her telling me, I hope I am not so stupid as to be ignorant of what's in a girl's mind. She will be very much surprised, and I am not so sure that she will obey."

"Mary—not obey!—I think you must be dreaming."

"It is all very easy to speak. Mary is most obedient about everything that is of no consequence: but this is of great consequence, John. And the girl is of age, though we have all got into the habit of treating her like a child. Why should she let her best chance drop, because you don't like it? I don't mean to say that it is much of a chance. But still a man like that may always get on, whereas a girl has very little likelihood, by herself, of getting on. And we can't always be here to look after her."

"I don't see why you should be so very determined on that subject," said the Squire, with a little irritation. "We are not so dreadfully aged, when all is said."

"No, we are not dreadfully aged, but we can't last forever. Suppose you were to be taken from us," said Mrs. Prescott, with placidity, "three girls would be a great responsibility for me: and suppose I were to go first, you would feel it still more. Indeed, I should be very sorry to refuse an offer for Mary. To see her with a husband to take care of her, would be a great comfort to me. Of course all that we can do must be for our own girls—and not too much for them," the mother said.

The Squire went out for his walk that day full of thought. He was a man who at the bottom of his heart was a kind man, and one with a conscience, a conscience of the kind which sometimes gives its possessor a great deal of trouble. He asked himself what was his duty to his sister's child? not to plunge her into poverty and the cares of life in order to get rid of the responsibility from his own shoulders. Oh no, that could never be his duty. But, at the same time, on the other hand, to leave her in the care of a good husband was the best thing that could happen to any girl. He knew enough of Mr. Asquith to be sure that he would be a good husband. He was a good man, a man quite superior to the ordinary type; though

41

the curate was not very popular at the Hall, still the Squire had perception enough to know this—that he was above the average, not at all a common man. And he must be very much in love with Mary, knowing that she had no money and no expectations, to have subjected himself to such a cross-examination as Mr. Prescott knew he had inflicted, on her account. Enlightened by his wife's remarks, the Squire thought the matter all over again from another point of view. The man was very poor, but then Mary was very simple in her tastes, and if the girl really preferred to marry him in a cottage, rather than to live on at the Hall, perhaps it was true that her uncle had no right to cross her. It was not exactly, he said to himself, as if he were her father. She had always been a docile little thing, but his wife seemed to think that there was a possibility that in this matter Mary might not be so docile, that she might take her own way; and if she did so there would be a breach in the family, and he would be compelled to withdraw his protection from her, and her mother's story might be enacted over again. Mary's mother's story had not been happy. She too had been asked in marriage by a poor man, and had been refused by her father. And she had run away with her lover, and had suffered more than Mr. Prescott liked to think of before she died. He said to himself now that perhaps if his father had consented, if they had tried to help Burnet on instead of letting him sink, things might have been different. Anyhow, he would never allow that episode to be repeated. And if Mary would marry Mr. Asquith, she must do it with the consent of her people, and everything that could be done must be done for her husband.

He went across the park to the rectory and consulted his brother Hugh on the subject, who was first amused and then shook his head. "I knew there would be mischief when I saw what kind of a man the fellow was," the rector said.

"What kind of a man! Why, he is not a lady's man at all, he plays no tennis, he never comes up in the afternoon, he seems to care nothing for society. Neither John nor the girls can make anything of him."

"Ah, that's the dangerous sort," said the Rev. Hugh, "there's no flutter in him. He settles on one, and there's an end of it. He's a terrible fellow to stick to a thing. Take my word for it, John, you'll have to give in."

The Squire liked this view of the subject less than his wife's view, and went home roused and irritated, vowing that he would not give in. But by that time he found Anna and Sophie discussing Mary's trousseau, and the whole household astir. "Of course she must have her things nice, and plenty of them, for one never knows whether she will be able to get any more when they're done," her cousins said. They were very good-natured. They never doubted the propriety of accepting the curate, and were, indeed, very strong in their mother's view of the subject—that seeing the uncertainty of life and the possibility any day of "something happening" to papa, to get Mary off the hands of the family and settled for life was a thing in every way to be desired. Mr. Prescott naturally did not contemplate the likelihood of "something happening" to himself with so much philosophy. But as they were all of one accord on the subject, and his own thoughts so much divided, he gave in, of course, as everybody knew he would do.

And the fact of Mr. Asquith's extreme poverty had its share, too, in quickening the marriage. A very rich man and a very poor man have nothing to wait for; they are alike in that—the rich, because his means are assured; the poor because he has no means to assure. There is nothing to wait for in either case. The rector gave Mr. Asquith privately to understand that he would be on the outlook for something better for him; and recommended the curate to do the same thing for himself. "For this may do to begin with, but it is poor pickings for two—and still less for three or four," Mr. Hugh Prescott said. And thus everything was arranged. John Prescott was the only one who took any unexpected part in the matter. He astonished them all one day by announcing suddenly that Mary must have a "thettlement." "A settlement?" said his father. "Poor child, there is nothing to settle either on one side or the other."

The conversation took place at luncheon one day, when Mary was at the rectory.

"That's just why there must be a thettlement," repeated John, with an obstinate air which he could put on when he chose, and of which they were all a little afraid.

"What nonsense!" said Mrs. Prescott; "her clothes are all there will be to settle, and they couldn't be taken from her, whatever might happen."

"I know what I'm thaying," said John. "She wants thomething to fall back upon, it he dies; for he may die, as well as another."

"That's very true," said Mr. Prescott, with some energy. He was relieved to feel that there was someone else to whom "something might happen," as well as himself.

"She must have a thouthand poundth," John said.

And then there arose a cry in the room, a sort of concerted yet unconcerted and unharmonious union of voices. The Squire made his exclamation in a deep growling bass. Mrs. Prescott came

43

in with a sort of alto, and the girls gave a short shrill shriek. A thousand pounds! thousands of pounds were not plentiful in Horton. Anna and Sophie themselves knew that very few would fall to their share, and neither of them had so much as a curate to make a living for her. They had been very willing to be liberal about the trousseau, but a thousand pounds! that was a different matter altogether. They all gazed with horror at the revolutionary who proposed this. John was not clever, as everybody knew; he looked still less clever than he was. He had pale blue eyes of a wandering sort, which did not look as if they were very secure in their sockets, and a long fair moustache drooping over the corners of his mouth. And he had a habit of sticking a glass in one eye, which fell out every minute or two and made a break in his conversation. Many people about Horton were of opinion that he was "not all there," but his family did not generally think so. At this moment, however, with one accord it occurred to them all that there was something not quite sane about John.

"Thir," said John to his father, "you needn't trouble if you've any objection. I mean to do it mythelf."

"Do it yourself! you must be out of your senses," cried his mother. "Where will you get a thousand pounds? I never heard such madness in all my life."

"I suppose he means to take it off his legacy," said the Squire, pale with emotion; "if you've got a thousand pounds to dispose of, you had better look a little nearer home. There's Percy always drawing upon me, and there's the house falling to pieces—"

"Or if you want to give it away, give it to your sisters, who have a great deal more to keep up with their little money than ever Mary will have," Mrs. Prescott said.

John did not say much. "I've thpoken to Bateman about the thettlement," he informed them, looking round dully with those unsteady eyes of his, with an awkward jerk of his head and twist of his face to arrest the fall of the eyeglass. The family, looking at him, were all exceptionally impressed with the dulness of John's appearance, the queerness of his aspect. Really he did not look as if he were "all there." But they were perfectly convinced they might move Horton House as soon as John, and that the settlement on Mary, which they all thought so completely unnecessary, was an accomplished thing.

Mary was more affected by it than she had ever been by anything in her life. John!—she said to herself that he had always taken her part, always been kind to her. Like the rest of the family, she had regretted sometimes that the dashing Percy, who was so much nicer to look at, so much more of a personage, so full of

44

spirit and life, had not been the elder brother. But Percy would have kept all his pounds to himself, everybody knew, though he had the air of being far more open-handed than his brother. Percy, however, on this emergency came out too in a very good light. He sent her a set of gold ornaments, a necklace and a bracelet of Indian work, for he was in India at the time, along with a delightful letter, asking how she could answer to herself for marrying first of all, she, who had always been the little one, and who could only be, Percy thought, about fifteen now. "Tell Asquith I think he is a very lucky fellow," Percy wrote. John never said a word, even at the wedding breakfast, when it was expected he should propose the health of the bride and bridegroom. All that he did was to get up from his seat, looking about him dully with those unsteady eyes, give a gasp like a fish, and then sit down again, his eyeglass rattling against his plate as it fell, which was the only sound he produced. But everybody knew what he meant, which was the great matter. And as for the "thettlement," the wisest man in England could not have arranged it more securely than John had done.

And so Mary and the curate were married in the late autumn, when the leaves were covering all the country roads, and the November fogs were coming on.

CHAPTER IX

"HAPPY EVER AFTER"

THE Asquiths, though they were so poor, got on very pleasantly at first. Mary had forty-five pounds a year from her thousand, and thought herself a millionaire; and Uncle Hugh gave the curate twenty pounds more in lieu of the lodgings, which were not adapted for a married man. With this twenty pounds they got a very pretty cottage—a little house which Mr. Prescott said was good enough for anybody; where, indeed, the widow of the last rector had lived till her death; and which had a pleasant garden, and was far above the pretensions of people possessing an income which even with these additions only came to a hundred and sixty-five pounds a year. The house was furnished for them, almost entirely by their kind friends—a very large contribution coming from the Hall, where there were many rooms that were never used, and even in the lumber-room many articles that were good to fill up. In this way the new married pair acquired some things that were very good and charming, and some things that were much the reverse. They got some Chippendale chairs, and an old cabinet which was in point of taste enough to make the fortune of any house; but they also got a number of things manufactured in the first half of the present century, of which the least said the better. They did not themselves much mind, and probably, being uninstructed, preferred the style of George IV. to that of Queen Anne.

And thus they lived very happily for two or three years. They lived very happy ever after, might indeed have been said of them, as if they had made love and married in a fairy tale. No words could have described their condition better. Mary, delivered from the small talk of the Horton drawing-room, and living in constant companionship with a man of education, whose tastes were more cultivated and developed than those of the race of squires, which was all she had hitherto known, brightened in intelligence as well as in happiness, and with the quick receptivity of her age grew into, without labour, that atmosphere of culture and understanding which is the fine fleur of education. She did not actually know much more, perhaps, than she had known in her former condition; but she began to understand all kinds of allusions, and to know what people meant when they quoted the poets, or referred to those great characters in fiction who are the most living people under the sun. She no longer required to have things explained to her of this kind. And as for the curate, it was astonishing how he brightened and softened, and became reconciled to the facts of existence; and found beauty and sweetness in those common paths which he had been disposed to look upon with hasty contempt. No two people in the world, perhaps, can live so much together, share everything so entirely, become one another, so to speak, in so complete a way as a country clergyman and his wife. Except the writing of his sermons, there was no part of his work into which Mr. Asquith's young wife did not enter; and even the sermons, which were all read to her before they were preached, were the better for Mary; for the curate was quick to note when her attention failed, when her eyelids drooped, as they did sometimes, over her eyes. She was far too loyal, and too much an enthusiast, you may be sure, ever to allow in words that those prelections were less than perfect; but Mr. Asquith was clever enough to see that sometimes her attention flagged. Once or twice, before the first year was out, Mary nodded while she listened—a delinquency which she denied almost furiously, with the wrath of a dove; and which was easily explained by the fact that she was at that moment "not very strong:" but which nevertheless Mr. Asquith, as he laughed and kissed her and said, "That was too much for you, Mary," took to heart. "Too much for me!" she cried; "if you mean far finer and higher than anything I could reach by myself, of course you are quite right, Henry; but only in that sense," the tears coming into her eyes in the indignation of her protest. The curate did not insist, nor try to prove to her that she had indeed dozed, which some men would have done. He was too delicate and tender for any such brutal ways of proving himself in the right; but, all the same, he laid that involuntary criticism to heart, to the great advantage of his preaching. Thus they did each other mutual good.

And what a beautiful life these two lived! I know a little pair in a little town, with not much more money than the Asquiths, and connections much less important, and surroundings much less pretty—a pair who have only a little house in a street, with unlovely houses of the poor about them, instead of comely cottages, who do very much the same, all honour to them! The Asquiths flung themselves upon that parish, and took the charge of it with a rush, out of the calm elderly hands which had for years managed it so easily. I do not undertake to say that they did no harm, or that they were always wise; nobody is that I have ever come in contact with: but if there is any finer thing in the world than to maintain a brave struggle with all that is evil on account of others, on account of the poor, who so often cannot help themselves, I don't know what it is. These two laid siege to all the strongholds of ill in the village—and evil, or the Evil One if you please to put it so, has many such strongholds—with all the energies of their being. They fought against wickedness, against disorder, against disease, against waste, and dirt, and drink; against the coarse habits and unlovely speech of the little rural place. They made a chivalrous attempt to turn all those rustics into ladies and gentlemen—into what is better, Christian men and women, into good and pure and thoughtful persons, considering not only their latter end, as the parson had always bidden them to do, but also their present living and all their habits and ways. The curate had been working very steadily, in this sense, since he came to Horton; but when he had, so to speak, Mary's young enthusiasm, her feminine practicalness, yet scorn of the practical and contempt of all the limits of possibility, poured into him, stimulating his own strength, the result was tremendous. The parish for a moment was taken by surprise, and in its astonishment was ready to consent to anything the young innovators desired. It would sin no more, neither be untidy any more; it would abandon the public-house and wash its babies' faces three times in the day; it would put something in the savings-bank every Saturday of its life, and open all its windows every morning, and pursue every smell to the death. All this and more it undertook in the consternation caused by that sudden onslaught: and for a little time, with those two active young people in constant circulation among the cottages, giving nobody any peace, scolding, praising, persuading, contrasting, encouraging, helping too in that incomprehensible way in which the poor do help the poor, a great effect was produced. As for going to church, that was the first and easiest point; and here Mary came in with her music, which the curate did not understand, influencing the choice of the hymns, and getting up choir practices, and heaven knows how many other seductions—artful temptations to the young to do well instead of doing ill—sweetnesses and pleasures to make delightful the narrow way.

"You think you are doing an immense deal," said Uncle Hugh, "but you'll find it won't last."

"Why shouldn't it last?" cried Mary. "They are so much happier in themselves. Don't you think a man must feel what a difference it makes when he comes home sober, and finds a nice supper waiting him on Saturday nights; and then to go out to church with all the children, neat and clean, round him, instead of lounging, dirty, at the door with his pipe?"

"Perhaps it is more comfortable," said the rector, shaking his head. "I should think so, certainly; but it isn't human nature, my dear. You will find that he will rather have his fling at the public-house, though he feels wretched next morning. He likes to see his children nice; but better still he likes his own pleasure. You'll find it won't last."

"We must be prepared for a few downfalls," said the curate. "I tell Mary that we must not expect everything to go on velvet. Some of them will fall away; but with patience, and sticking to it, and never giving in——"

"Never giving in!" cried Mary. "Why, uncle, you don't suppose I am so silly as to think we could build Rome in a day. We quite look for failures now and then," she said, with her bright face. "We should almost be disappointed if we had no failures; shouldn't we, Henry? for then it wouldn't look real; but with patience and time everything can be done."

The rector only shook his head. He did not say, as he might have done, that it was very presumptuous of these young people to think they could do more in a few months than he had done in his long incumbency. The rector's wife was very strong on this point, and quite angry with Mary and the curate for their ridiculous hopes; but Mr. Prescott himself felt, perhaps, that his reign had been an indolent one, and that he had not done all he might. But he shook his head; for, after all, though he had been indolent, he knew human nature better than they did. He was not angry with them; but he had seen such crusades before, and had various sad experiences as to the dying out of enthusiasm, and the failure of hope. And the rector, who was a kind man in his heart, knew through the ladies of the family that the time was approaching when Mary would be "not very strong," and apt to flag in other matters besides that of listening to her husband's sermon. And he knew, also, that the conditions of life would change for them; that the young wife would find work of her own to do, which could not be put aside for the parish; and that "patience and time," on which they calculated, were just what they would not have to give: for when babies began to come, and all their expenses were increased, how were they to go on with one hundred and sixty-five pounds a year? The rector said to himself that he would not discourage them, that they should do what they would as long as they could. But he foresaw that the time would come when Mr. Asquith would be compelled to seek another curacy with a little more money, and when Mary, instead of being the good angel of the parish, would have to be nurse and superior servant-of-all-work at home.

"Poor things!" he said to his wife. "It is sad when you have to acknowledge that you are no longer equal to the task you have set for yourself."

"I don't call them poor things," said Mrs. Prescott. "I think them very presuming, Hugh, after you have spent so many years here, to think they can bring in new principles and make a reformation in a single day."

"We might have done more, my dear. We have taken things very quietly; most likely we could have done more."

"You are as bad as they are, with your humility!" cried the rector's wife. "I have no patience with you. What have you left undone that you ought to have done? I am sure you've always been at their beck and call, rising up out of your warm bed to go and visit them in the middle of the night, when you have been sent for—more like a country practitioner than a beneficed clergyman! And though I say it that perhaps shouldn't say it, never one has been sent away, as you know, that came in want to our pantry door. And as for lyings-in, and those sort of things——" cried the country lady.

"We needn't go into details. As for your part of it, my dear, I know that's always been well done," said the politic rector. "Anyhow, don't let us say anything to discourage the Asquiths. It's always a good thing to stir a parish up."

"It's like those revivalists," said Mrs. Prescott—"a great fuss, and then everything falling back worse than before."

"Oh no! not worse than before: somebody is always the better for it. I like a good stirring up."

All this was very noble of the rector, who, if ever he had stirred up the parish, had ceased to do it long ago. Perhaps he was a little moved by the fervent conviction of the curate and the curate's wife that in their little day, and with the small means at their command, they could do so much; at all events, he let them have their way and try their best. And a great deal of work was done, with an effect by which they were greatly delighted and elated in the first year.

But then came the time when Mary was "not very strong," and the choir practices and various other things had to be given up—not entirely given up, for the schoolmaster and his daughter made an attempt to keep them on, which was more trying to the nerves and patience of the invalid than if they had ceased altogether. For jealousies arose, and the different parties thought themselves entitled to carry their grievances to Mrs. Asquith, even when she was very unfit for any disturbance; and everything was very heavy on the curate's shoulders during that period of inaction which was compulsory on Mary's part. They had undertaken so much, that when one was withdrawn the other could not but break down with overwork. However, there was presently a re-beginning; and Mary, smiling and happier than ever, prettier than ever, and full of a warmer enthusiasm still, came again to the charge. She understood the poor women, the poor mothers, so much better now, she declared. Even the curate himself was not such an instructor as that little three-weeks-old baby, which did nothing but sleep, and feed, and grow. That was a teacher fresh from heaven; it threw light on so many things, on the very structure of the world, and how it hung together, and the love of God, and the ways of men. Mary thought she had never before so fully understood the prayer which is addressed to Our Father: she had not known all it meant before: and the curate, indescribably softened, touched, melted out of all perception of the hardness, feeling more than ever the sweetness of life, received this ineffable lesson too.

And so the crusade against the powers of evil was taken up again, with all the new life of this little heavenly messenger to stimulate them; but not quite so much of the more vulgar strength, the physical power, the detachedness and freedom. Mary had to be at home with the baby so often and so long. And the curate had so strong a bond drawing him in the same direction, to make sure that all was going well. But still the parish did not suffer in those young and happy years.

CHAPTER X

THE LIGHT OF COMMON DAY

EVEN in the quietest lives the first few years of married life are apt to bring changes: the ideal dies off, with its fairy colours; the realities of ordinary existence come with a leap upon the surprised young people, to whom everything has been enveloped in the glory and the brightness of a dream. That plunge into the matter-of-fact is often more trying to the husband—who rarely sees the bride of his visions drop into the occupations of the housewife and the mother without a certain pang—than to the young woman herself, who in the pride and delight of maternity finds a still higher promotion, and to whom the commonest cares, the most material offices, which she would have shrunk from a little while before, become half divine. But when the house is very poor to begin with, and there is no margin left for enlargements, this inevitable change is more deeply felt. By the time the third child arrived, the Asquiths had changed their ideas about many things. Mary's help in the parish was now very fitful. She still accomplished what was a great deal "for her:" but there had been no conditions or limits to her labours in those early days, when she had worked like a second curate, bearing her full share of everything. These were the days in which so many things had been undertaken, more than any merely mortal curate could keep up; and in the meantime there had been a great many disappointments in the parish. Even before Mary's powers failed, the influence of the new impulse was over. The people had got accustomed to all the many things that were being done for them: they were no longer taken by surprise. The ancient vis inertia— that desire to be let alone which is so strong in the English character—came uppermost once more. "Oh, here's this botherin' practice again!" the boys and girls began to say; or, "It's club night, but I ain't a-going. Them as gets the good of the money can come and fetch it!"—for the village people by this time had got it well into their heads that the custody of their pennies and sixpences was in some occult way to the curate's advantage. And so in one way after another, ground was lost. Mr. Asquith got fagged and worn out in his efforts to do more than one man could do, without the help which had borne him up so triumphantly at first; he was deeply discouraged by the defection of so many; and he felt to the bottom of his soul the triumph in the eyes of Mrs. Prescott, at the rectory, who had always said nothing would come of it. The rector, for his part, would not show any triumph. He had behaved very well throughout; he had not resented the curate's attempts to improve upon all his own ways, and do more than ever had been done before in Horton. And now when the fervour of these first reformations began to fail, he did not say, "I told you so," as so many would have done. He was very moderate, very temperate, rather consoling than aggravating the disappointment. "Human nature is always the same," he said. "Even when you get it stirred up for a time, it reclaims its right to do wrong—and yet all good work tells in the long run," Mr. Prescott said, which was very good-natured of him, and was indeed straining a point; for he was by no means so sure that in the long run these Quixotic exertions did tell. But Mrs. Prescott was not so forbearing. "You might have known from the beginning this was how it would be," she said to Mary. "You young people think you are the only people who have ever attempted anything; but it isn't so—it's quite the contrary. We have all tried what we could do, and we've all been disappointed. I could have told you so from the first, if you had shown any inclination to be guided by me!"

"Oh, Aunt Jane!" cried Mary, "it all went on beautifully at first. It is my fault, that have not kept up as I ought to have done. If I hadn't been such a poor creature, everything would have gone well."

"There is something in that," said Mrs. Prescott, who had never had any babies. "It is always a sad thing when a young woman has so many children——"

"Aunt Jane!" cried Mary, almost with a scream. She gathered the little new baby to her bosom, and over its downy little head glared at her childless aunt. "As if they were not the most precious things in life—as if they were not God's best gift! as if we could do without any one of them!"

"Perhaps not, my dear, now they are here," said Mrs. Prescott; "but you may let your friends say that it would have been much better for you if they had not come so fast."

To this Mary could not make any reply, though her indignation was scarcely diminished. She was, indeed, very indignant on this point. All of these ladies—her aunt at the Hall and the girls, as well as her aunt at the rectory—spoke and looked as if Mary was no better than a victim, helplessly overwhelmed with children; whereas she was a proud and happy mother, thinking none of them fit to be compared with her in her glory. That they should venture to pity her, and say poor Mary! she, who was in full possession of all that is most excellent in life, was almost more than the curate's wife could bear. Her two little boys and her little girl were her jewels as they were those of the Roman woman whom Mary had heard of, but whom she would have thought it too high-flown to quote. She felt, all the same, very much like that classical matron. Anna and Sophie were very proud of their diamond pins, which even for diamonds were poor things; and they had the impertinence to pity her and her three children! Mary fumed all the time they paid her their visits, which had the air of being visits of condolence rather than of congratulation; and in her weakness cried with vexation and indignation after they had left. The curate came in before those angry tears were dried, and her agitated feelings burst forth. "They come to me and pity me," she cried, "till I don't know how to endure them! Oh, Harry, I wish we were not so near my relations! Strangers daren't be so nasty to you as your relations!" Mary sobbed, with the long-pent-up feeling, which in that moment of feebleness she could not restrain.

"My dearest, never mind them," he said soothingly. And then, after a pause, with some hesitation,—"Mary, this gives me courage to say what I never liked to say before. Don't you find, even with your own little income, dear, which I was so anxious should not be touched, and with all the advantages here, that it is very difficult to make both ends meet?"

"Oh, Harry! I have been trying to keep it from you. I didn't want to burden you with that too. Difficult! it is impossible! I must give Betsy warning. I have been making up my mind to it. After all, it is only pride, you know, for she is very little good. I have had most of the work to do myself all the time. I must give her warning as soon as I am well—or rather, we must try to find her a place, which is the best way."

"What?" cried the curate. "Betsy, the only creature you have to do anything for you! No, no. I cannot allow that."

"The housekeeping is my share," said Mary, with a smile; "now that I can do so little in the parish, I may at least be of use at home. And if you only knew how little good she is! She can't even amuse little Hetty, and Jack won't go to her!" These frightful details Mary gave with the temerity they deserved. "I'll tell you what I am going to do. There are the Woods, who have always been so nice, so regular at school, and attentive about the club. I mean to have Rosie, the eldest, to come in for an hour or two in the morning to look after the children while I get things tidy; and then Mrs. Wood herself will come on Saturdays and give everything a good clean up: and you will see we shall get on beautifully," Mary said, smiling upon him with her dewy eyes, which were still wet. But the irritation had all died away, and in the pallor of her recent pangs, and the sacredness of her motherhood, no queen of a poet's imagination could have looked more sweet.

"Oh, Mary, my darling!" cried the poor curate in his love and compunction. "To think I should have brought you to this!"

"To what?" said Mary radiant, "to the greatest happiness in life, to do everything for one's own? Oh! Harry, I am afraid I have not the self-devotion a clergyman's wife ought to have. I was happy to work in the parish—but, dear, if you won't despise me very much—I think I am happier to work for the children and you."

What could the poor man do? He kissed her and went away humiliated, yet happy. That he should have to consent to be served by her in the homeliest practical ways—she, who was his love and his lady—had something excruciating in it; and to think that his love should have brought her to this, and that he should have foreseen it, and yet done it in the weakness of his soul! But when he went back to that, the curate could not be sorry either that he had loved Mary, or that he had told her his love, or married her. She was not sorry—God bless her!—but radiant and happy as the day, and more sweet, and more sacred, and more beautiful than she had been even in her girlhood. What could he say? He would not even disturb that exquisite moment by telling her of the change that he was beginning to contemplate. Things could wait at least for a few days.

But when she told him that she had given Betsy warning, the curate did speak. "I have done it," she said, partly by way of excuse for bringing in the tea herself, which she did, panting a little, but smiling over the tray. "We shall be so much better off with Mrs. Wood coming in one day in the week. Then we shall really have the satisfaction of knowing that everything is clean for once, and no little spy in the house to report to everybody what we have for dinner; but we must try and get her another place, Harry; for though the children don't like her, and I should never recommend her for a nursery, there are some things that she can do."

"Some things you have taught her to do," Mr. Asquith said.

"So much the more credit to me," said Mary, laughing, "for she is not very easy to teach."

It was evening, and the children were in bed and all quiet. The little creature last born lay all covered up in the sitting-room beside them, in a cradle, which the ladies at the Hall, notwithstanding their indignation at his appearance, had trimmed with muslin and lace and made very ornamental: and Mary was glad to put herself in the rocking-chair which her cousin John had given her, and lie back a little and rest. "One never knows," she said, "how pleasant it is to rock, till one knows what work is. But, Harry, you are over-tired, you don't care for your tea."

"I care a great deal more for seeing you tired," he said. "Mary, I want to speak to you about something very serious. Would it break your heart, my dearest, if we were to go away from Horton? That is the question I didn't venture to ask the other day."

"Break my heart! when the children are well, and you? What a question to ask! Nothing could break my heart," cried Mary, with a delightful laugh, "so long as all is right with you."

And then he told her that another curacy had been offered him, a curacy in a large town. It would be very different from Horton. He would be under the orders of a very well-known clergyman, a great organiser, a man who was very absolute in his parish, instead of being free to do almost anything he pleased, as under Uncle Hugh's mild sway. And he would have a great deal of work, but within bounds and limits, so that he would know what was expected from him, without having the general responsibility of everything. And though he would be under the rector, yet he would be over several younger curates, and in his way a sort of vice-bishop too. "But you must remember," he said, "that we shall have to live in a street without any garden, with very little fresh air. It will be quite town, not even like a suburb—nothing but stone walls all round you."

Mary's countenance fell. "Oh, Harry! that will not be good for the children."

"I believe there is a park in which the children can walk," he said, upon which Mary brightened once more.

"In that case, I don't mind the other things," she said, rocking softly in her chair; "but, Harry, how shall you like to be dictated to, and told everything that you have to do?"

"I should like anything," he said, "that gave you a little more comfort, my poor Mary. There is two hundred and fifty a year——"

He said it with solemnity, as was right—"Two hundred and fifty a year." Few are the curates who rejoice in such an income. Mary brought her chair down upon the floor with a sound which but lightly emphasised her astonishment and awe. These feelings were so strong in her mind that they had to be expressed before pleasure came.

"And you really have this offered to you, Harry? offered, without looking for it?"

"Yes," said the curate, with the hush and wonder of humility, feeling that he could not account for such a piece of good fortune.

"That shows," cried she, "how much you are appreciated,

how you are understood. Oh, Harry! the world is wonderfully kind and right-feeling, after all."

"Yes," he said, "sometimes; there are a great many kind people in the world. And you don't mind it, my darling? you don't mind leaving Horton and all your relations, and the neighbourhood you have lived in all your life?"

"Mind it!" she cried, and paused a little, and dried her eyes, which were full. "Harry," she said, with a little solemnity, "I think when people marry and have a family of their own, it is always a little like the beginning of a new world; don't you think so? Everything is changed. It seems natural to go to a new place, to make a real new start, more natural than to stay where one has always been. Then, when they grow up, there will be openings for the boys; and Hetty will be able to get a good education. Mind it! I am sure it is the right thing."

"I am very glad, dear. I feared you might have doubts about leaving the parish."

"After all," said Mary, "we have done everything we could for the parish; and perhaps a little novelty would be good for them now. Uncle Hugh will be very particular in choosing a very good man to succeed you. And we have done everything we could; perhaps a new curate who is a novelty may be better for the parish too."

CHAPTER XI

THE FIRST CHANGE

THERE was a good deal of difficulty made among the relations about this removal. The ladies particularly were very decided on the subject. Who would look after Mary? who would see that she did not do too much, that she took proper nourishment, that she had from time to time a new gown, if she went away? "She will never think of these things for herself," said Mrs. Prescott at the Hall to Mrs. Prescott at the Rectory. "She will give everything to the children. She will think of him and them, and never of herself."

"But I don't see what we can do," said the clergyman's wife. "We cannot keep them here against their will. It is a far better income than Hugh can afford to give. And with children coming so fast, they will soon have to think of education and all that. I don't like it any more than you do," added the clerical lady, "but what can we do?"

They, however, all felt that Mary's satisfaction in the change was ungrateful and almost unnatural.

"You will never know the advantages you have had till you go away," her aunt said to her. "You have always had some one to refer to, some one to take you out a little and make you forget your cares. But among strangers it will be different. You don't know how different it will be."

Perhaps Mary was a little ungrateful. She did not estimate at their due value the dinners at the Hall to which she and the curate had often gone quite unwillingly, though the givers of these entertainments thought it was a great thing for the young couple to have somebody who was always ready to ask them. Young couples are apt to be ungrateful in this way, to think little of the home invitations, and to prefer their own company to that of their relatives; and Mary had not been better than others in this respect. She and Mr. Asquith had said to each other that it was a bore when they went to the Hall to dine. They had said to each other that their evenings at home were much more delightful. Though Mary at this period would not have believed it possible, yet there were moments in later years when they would have found it very agreeable to return to those old dinners at the Hall: but of that she was at present quite unaware. She was, indeed, it must be allowed, a little too exultant and happy about her move. To think that this advancement had been offered to the curate, such an important post, so much superior to anything that could have been hoped for at this early stage, elated her beyond measure. And the increased income was a great thing. Giving up at once, and with great ease, the idea of training young servants to such perfection that people should come far and near to compete for a maid who had been with Mrs. Asquith, which was her first ideal, Mary rejoiced in the prospect of getting a real servant, a woman who knew her work, "a thorough good maid-of-all-work," she said with importance, as if she had been speaking of a groom of the chambers. "Oh, the relief it will be just to tell her what has to be done, without having to show her everything!" Mrs. Asquith said.

"But you used to think it would be so much better to train one to your own ways," the curate replied, not being used to so rapid a change of principle.

"Ah, I have learned something myself since then," said Mary. And so she had—the first lesson in life, which has so many and such hard lessons, especially for those who study in the school of poverty. Poor Mary thought her troubles were over now. She even formed dreams of having a little nursemaid to wheel out the perambulator, Two hundred and fifty eked out by that forty-five of her own! Why, it was a princely income; and privation and discomfort, she fully believed, were now to be things of the past.

There was some difficulty in getting the furniture transported to the new place, for some of it was very heavy and large, having come direct, as has been said, from the lumber rooms and unused part of the Hall. The curate proposed with diffidence that these lordly articles should be sold, and others more suitable bought, to save the expense of carriage; but Mary was shocked by the suggestion. "They are all presents," she said; "we couldn't, oh, we couldn't, Harry, without hurting their feelings. It would look as if we thought those things not good enough for us that were good enough for them."

"But they were not good enough for them, or they would not have been given to us," said the curate, a speech which he repented immediately, for Mary would not have such a reproach thrown upon her relations; and her husband ate his words and explained that it was because the great mahogany sideboard, etc., were too good for a curate's little house that he wished to dispose of them, which mended matters. And even now everybody was very kind. Uncle Hugh insisted on adding twenty pounds to the last quarter's income for travelling expenses, which, considering that his curate was deserting him, was liberal indeed; and the Squire was not behind in liberality. There was perhaps a little of the feeling on the part of the richer relations that they were thus washing their hands of Mary, setting her up once for all, so that she never could have any excuse for saying that her mother's brothers had not done their duty by her. Neither of these kind men, who were really fond of her in their way, would have said this even to themselves. But it must be remembered that she had chosen for herself, and contrary to their advice, and that she had been fully warned of the poverty which was likely to be her lot, and that they could not always stand between her and its penalties. But if this was their feeling, they were at least very kind and liberal in this final setting out, which also was her own doing or her husband's doing, and no way suggested by any desire of theirs to get rid of her. And her aunt and the girls urged upon her the necessity of writing, and keeping them fully informed of all that happened. "Write every week," said Mrs. Prescott at the Hall; "if you don't make a habit of it, you will fall out of it altogether. Now, Mary, remember, once a week."

"Don't let us hear of the new babies only through the newspapers," said Mrs. Prescott at the Rectory.

"Oh, Aunt John, of course I shall write every week, or oftener. Oh, Aunt Hugh, how could you suppose such a thing? and perhaps there will be no more babies," Mary said.

She was a little tearful as she bade them all good-bye, remembering then, with a touch of compunction, how kind they had always been; but all the same she was radiant, setting out upon life for the first time, setting out fairly upon the new world, upon her own career, without any of the old traditions. Heretofore, though she had attained the dignity of marriage and maternity, Mary had not felt the greater splendour of independence. Now she was going out with no head but her husband, and no beaten paths in which she must tread. They were going to trace their own way through the world, their own way and that of their children, the way of a new family, a new house, a new nation and tribe, distinct among the other tribes, not linked on, a subsidiary sept to the tribe of the Prescotts. Perhaps there was a little ingratitude in this, too, as there is in every erection of a new standard; but they did not see it from that point of view. She was radiant in the glory of her separate beginning, glad to throw off the thraldom of natural subjection, just as they were perhaps glad to wash their hands of her and her concerns. Neither expressed the feeling, or would have acknowledged it; but it was a natural feeling enough on both sides.

John was the last of the Prescotts to bid his cousin good-bye. He came in at a very inappropriate moment, when all the things were packed, and the children were having their hats and hoods tied on, and making a great noise in inarticulate baby excitement, delighted with the commotion. He strolled in at this moment probably because it was the worst he could have chosen, and stood looking at the emptied and desolate cottage, and the family all in their travelling dresses, waiting for the carriage which was coming from the Hall to take them to the station. "I've come to thay good-bye," said John, looking all about him, as if with a desire to see whether they were carrying any of the fixtures away.

"Oh, John, how kind of you," said Mary, "though we are in such a confusion: there is not a chair to ask you to sit down in."

"I don't want to thit down," said John. And he stood for a little longer gazing round him until Mr. Asquith had gone out to look for the carriage, which was late—or at least, so they thought in their anxiety, to be in good time for the train. This appeared to be what John wanted, for he said more quickly than usual, "I don't want to thit down; I want to thay thomething before you go away."

"What is it, Cousin John? Oh, I am in such a confusion——"

"Yes, you are in a great confuthion," said John solemnly; and then he added after another pause, "if you should ever want anything down there," pointing with his thumb vaguely over his shoulder, "write to me."

"Oh, thank you, Cousin John; but we sha'n't want anything, I hope. Oh, there's the carriage," Mary cried; "I hear it at last."

John stood by gravely shaking his head, his mouth a little open, his moustache drooping. "Thingth are always wanted," he said solemnly. "Write to me."

Mary recounted this little incident to her husband after they had established themselves comfortably in the railway carriage, and had waved their hands for the last time to the people assembled to bid them good-bye, and were dashing along over the country, a family detached and set afloat in the world, a new race setting forth to conquer the earth. A sort of atmosphere of excitement, of elation, of novelty, and enthusiasm was about them, so that they were a little sorry for the homelier people going about quietly, looking out of the windows of calm country houses, standing at cottage doors, all in their ordinary way. To be so far out of their ordinary way, in such a rush and whirl of unaccustomed sensation, seemed to them a superiority—an elevation such as the dwellers in every-day life might well be envious of. Mary told her husband about John, and they both laughed, in their superiority of happiness, at the awkward good fellow who had thought it right to make this overture, which it was so little likely they would ever take advantage of. Mary herself laughed, she could not help it: but she said "Don't laugh at him,

61

Harry; it was a kind thought, a little out of place, perhaps, but we must not judge him by ordinary rules. He may be silly, but he is so kind. Don't! It hurts me when you laugh at John;" but she laughed herself just a little, softly, under her breath.

"I am not laughing at him," said the curate; "he is by far the best of the lot, and worth a dozen of that Percy you all make such a fuss about; but I don't think you'll write to him to ask his help—at least, I hope not."

"Harry!" she said with indignation, as if the mere idea of wanting help at all, she his wife, and he the senior curate of St. John's, Radcliffe, was a suggestion so ridiculous as almost to be an offence. And in this spirit they pursued their happy journey across England to the other side of the kingdom, with, not their flocks and herds, like the patriarchs, but what comes to the same thing, their furniture and their boxes and their children, to settle down in the well-watered plain, in the land flowing with milk and honey, in which their career and their surroundings were to be all their own.

I cannot follow all the details of their history step by step. St. John's, Radcliffe, did not turn out to be paradise, nor did Mary find boundless capabilities in two hundred and fifty pounds a year. After the first twelvemonth, the cares of life began again to make themselves felt, and fatigue and occasional low spirits chequered their career which nevertheless they still felt to be a fine career. They stayed six years altogether in this place, and left it for what was supposed to be a much better position, with an increased number of children and considerable cheerfulness, though not perhaps with the same elation which had characterised their first setting out. The second post the curate obtained was that of locum tenens to an invalid rector, and hopes were expressed, that in case of good service, if the rector should die, the patron's choice would most probably fall upon the temporary incumbent. The prospect was delightful, though sufficiently tempered by doubt to make Mr. Asquith hesitate about relinquishing St. John's. But then it is an understood thing that curates should not consider themselves permanent incumbents; and there were evidences that the rector would like a change, though he would not send so deserving a man with so large a family away. The way the family went on increasing was wonderful, was almost criminal, some people said. Only poor people, and poor clergymen above all, permitted themselves such expansion; and what was to become of all those helpless little things, spectators asked who never attempted to solve their own question. Nevertheless, they got on somehow as large families do. Mary had always a smile and thanksgiving for every new-comer, considering it as a gift of God, and thinking it hard that the poor little intruder should not have a welcome. And that, I confess, is my idea too, though it is a little out of fashion. But life was not much of a holiday under such circumstances, as will be easily understood; and Mary learnt a great many lessons, and went on learning, and had to contradict herself and change her mind over and over again as the years went on. She had begun bravely to write every week, as her aunt charged her; but gradually that good habit had fallen into disuse; and as the Asquiths moved from one place to another, they lost sight of their relations, hearing from them only once in a way, when anything remarkable happened, and at last coming to the pitch that they never heard at all. In sixteen years, which is the time at which I take up my curate and his Mary in their daily life again, a great many things had happened. "The girls" at Horton had both married, one a Frenchman, who took her to live abroad; another an officer in India. The old people at the Hall were both dead. Uncle Hugh was an invalid, living mostly in Italy for his health. And all that belonged to Mary's youthful life had fallen out of sight. This was the state of affairs in the curate's house, when Hetty, the eldest girl, the best child that ever was born, reached her sixteenth birthday: a day which was celebrated by a proposal at once exciting, fortunate, and painful, as shall be now set forth.

CHAPTER XII

THE ELDEST CHILD

HETTY was sixteen that day. There were nine younger than she was. When these words are said, coupled with the fact already told that Hetty was the best child that ever was born, they may not throw much light upon her character—and yet they will show with tolerable distinctness what her external position was. She was the best little nurse, the best housemaid, the most handy needle-woman, the most careful little housekeeper in all Summerfield, which, as everybody knows, is a suburb of the great town of Rollinstock, in the middle of England. She could make beef-tea and a number of little invalid dishes, better, and more quickly and more neatly, than any one else that ever was known, for, naturally, her mother was often in a condition to want a little care; and the children had every childish malady under the sun, all of them together, in the most friendly, comfortable way, and never were any the worse. Something defended them which does not defend little groups of two or three in richer nurseries. They sickened and got well again, as a matter of course, whenever there was any youthful epidemic about. They were altogether quite an old-fashioned family, having all the complaints that children ought to have, but remaining impervious to all the imperfections of drainage and all the dangers of brain exhaustion. Their blood was never poisoned, nor their nerves shattered. They got ill and got well again, as children used to do in old days. And Hetty, without ever setting foot in a hospital or having any instruction, was one of those heaven-born little nurses who used to flourish in novels and poetry, and who, as a matter of fact, were found in many families in those days when it was the fashion to believe that it was a woman's first duty to serve and care for those who were her own. Hetty was not aware of any individual existence of hers apart from her family. They were all one, and she was the eldest, which is a fact confusing, perhaps, to the arithmetical faculties, but quite easy to the heart.

The family, by this time, was at its fourth or fifth removal. Mr. Asquith had not got the living when the invalid rector died to whom he was locum tenens; and if his heart ever grew sick of his toils and poorly rewarded labour, it was at the moment when the family had to turn out of the nice old-fashioned rectory which they had been allowed to occupy during that period of expectation. For one moment the curate had asked himself what was the use of it all, and had said, in the bitterness of his heart, that his work never had time to come to anything, and that all the fond hopes of doing good, and bettering the poor, and helping the weak, with which he had set out in life, had come to nought. Women are perhaps not so apt to come to such a conclusion, and though Mary was aware, too, of many a defeat and downfall, she did her best to console him. "And then there are the children," she said. The poor man, at that moment, felt that the children were the last aggravation of his trouble, so many helpless creatures to be dragged after him wherever he had to go. He looked at the hand which his wife had put upon his to comfort him. What a pretty hand it had once been! and now how scarred and marked with work, its pretty whiteness gone, its texture spoiled, the forefinger half sewed away, the very shape of it, once so taper and delicate, lost. "Oh," he said, "what a hard life I have brought upon you, Mary! To think if I had only had more command of myself, you might never have known any trouble!"

Mary replied with a shriek, "Do you mean if we had never married? I think you have gone out of your senses, Harry."

"I think I almost have, with trouble," said the poor man. And yet, after all, his trouble was not half hers. It was she who had to bear the children, and nurse them, and have all the fatigue of them; it was she who had to scheme about the boys' shoes and their schooling, and how to get warm things for the winter, and to meet the butchers and bakers when they came to suggest that they had heavy payments to make: and to bear all these burdens with a smile, lest he should break down. When she had sent him out, frightened into better spirits by the ridiculous absurdity of the suggestion that they might never have married (which was much the same as saying that this world might never have been created; and that, no doubt, would have saved a great deal of trouble), Mary made her little explosion in her turn. "It is much papa knows!" she cried. "I wonder if he had our work for a day or two what he would think of it. And now we shall have to pack into a small house again, where he can have no quiet room for his study. Oh, Hetty, what shall we do? What shall we do?"

Hetty kissed her mother, with soft arms round her neck. "We must just do the best we can, mamma," Twelve-years-old said, "and don't you notice nothing turns out so bad as it seems?" added the little philosopher. Hetty, like her mother before her, had a wholesome love of change, and a persistent hope in the unknown. And on the whole, barring their little breakings down, they all appeared with quite cheerful faces in their new place; and life

65

turned out always to be livable wherever they went. The spectacle of their existence was a much more wonderful one to spectators than to themselves; for the lookers-on did not know the alleviations, the dear love among them, which was always sweet, the play of the children, which was never kept under by any misfortune, the household jests and pleasantries. They got a joke even out of the visits of the butcher and baker, those awful demands which it was so difficult to meet, and called the taxman Mr. Lillyvick, and made fun of the coal-merchant. And then, somehow or other, the kind heavens only knew how, everybody was paid in the long run, and life was never unsweet.

And now Hetty was sixteen. She was growing out of the lankness of early girlhood into a pretty creature—pretty with youth, and sweetness, and self-unconsciousness, and that exquisite purity of innocence which does not know what evil is. I am not aware that she had a single feature worth any one's notice. Her eyes were as clear as two little stars, but so are most eyes at sixteen. She was not what her mother had been, but rather what all good mothers would wish their children to be: something a little more than her mother, mounted upon the stepping-stone of Mary's cheerful troubled existence to the next grade, with something in her Mary had not, perhaps got from her father, perhaps, what I think most likely, straight out of heaven. Mary had not been at all afraid of life, out of sweet ignorance and want of thought; but Hetty knew it, and was not afraid. She had her dreams, like every creature of her age, her thoughts of what she would do and be when her hour came; but they never involved the winning of anything, save perhaps rest and comfort for those she loved. To Hetty life was a very serious thing. She knew nothing at all of its pleasures,—probably the defect in her, if she had a defect (and she must have had, for everybody has), was that she despised these pleasures. When she read in her story-books of girls whose dreams were of balls and triumphs, and who were angry with fate and the world when they did not obtain their share of these delights, Hetty would throw back her head with disdain. "I am sure girls are not like that," she would say.

"Oh yes, Hetty, girls are like that!" Mary would reply. "I remember crying my eyes out because Anna and Sophie went to the hunt ball without me."

This would generally lead to recollections of the house which Mary now called, with a sigh, "my dear old home," and of all the Prescotts, "the girls," and dashing Percy, and "kind old John." The children had all heard of Cousin John: how his eyeglass was always dropping from his eye (so well known was this trait in the family that little Johnny had got into the trick of it, and would stick a piece of paste-board in his little eye, which when it fell always produced a laugh), and his light moustache drooping at the corners, and his lisp, and how he said "Write to me," if anything was ever wanted.

"And did you ever write to him, mamma?" the children would cry. And then Mary would explain that she had never written so often as she ought, and impress the lesson upon them always to keep on writing when they might happen to be away, or they were sure to be sorry for it afterwards. "But did you write when you wanted anything?" said Janey, the second daughter, who was very inquisitive.

"No, of course mother didn't. As if we were going to take things from relations, like the Browns!" cried Harry, with a flush of scorn. Harry was a very proud boy, who suffered by reason of the short sleeves of his jacket and the short legs of his trousers, as none of the rest did. Mary shook her head at this, and said there was nothing wrong in taking things from relations when they were kind.

"But I never did," she said. "Sometimes I have thought I ought to have done it; but I never did. He married, and I never heard anything of him afterwards, and she was a stranger to me. It was that chiefly that kept me back. I have not heard anything of him for about a dozen years. And whether he has sold Horton, or what has become of it, I don't know. It is such a wrong thing not to write," she said, returning to her moral; "be sure you always keep up the habit of writing whenever you go away."

This, however, has kept us a long time from Hetty's birthday. Mr. Asquith had quite recently settled at Summerfield, the western suburb of Rollinstock, at the time when Hetty completed her sixteenth year. I say settled, for it was only now that our curate ceased to be a curate, and became, not, alas! rector or vicar, but incumbent of the new district church lately built in that flourishing place. It was a flourishing church also, and everything promised well; but as the endowment was very small, and the incumbent's income was dependent upon a precarious addition of pew-seats, offertories, etc., it was not a very handsome one for the moment, though promising better things to come. And the fact that he was independent, subject to no superior in his own parish, was sweet to a man who had been under orders so long. This beginning was very hopeful in every way. And Mr. Asquith had the character of being a very fine preacher, likely to bring all the more intellectual residents of the place, the great railway people—for the town was quite the centre of an immense railway system—and all the engineers and persons who thought something of themselves, to his church. This prospect encouraged them all, though perhaps the income was not very much better than that of a curacy. And there were good schools for the boys. The one thing that Mary sighed after was something of the higher education, of which everybody talks nowadays, for Hetty. But perhaps it is wrong to call it the higher education. No Greek nor even Latin did Mary desire for her daughter—these things were incompatible with her other duties—but a little music, a little of what had been called accomplishments in Mary's own day! In all likelihood these things would have done Hetty no manner of good,—no, nor the Latin either, nor even Greek. There are some people to whom education, in the common sense of the word, is unnecessary. But Mary had a mother's little vanity for her child. Hetty was but a poor performer on the piano; and her mother thought she had a great deal of taste, if it could but be cultivated. But music lessons are dear, especially in a town where rich mercantile folk abound. Alas! the boys' education was a necessity; the girls had to go to the wall.

The schoolroom tea was a very magnificent meal on Hetty's birthday. Sixteen seemed a great age to the children. It was as if she had attained her majority. Mary had got her a new white frock for the occasion made long. It was her first long dress, her toga, her robe of womanhood. And there was a huge cake, largely frosted over with sugar, if not very rich inside, out of regard for the digestion of the little ones. And they were all as happy over this tea as if it had been a sumptuous meal, with champagne flowing. They had not finished when Mr. Rossmore was announced, who was the Vicar of Rollinstock and a great personage. Mr. Rossmore was very kind; he was fond of children, and liked, as he said, to see them happy. And he sent a message from the drawing-room (in which there were still lingerings of the old Horton furniture), into which he had been ushered solemnly, to ask if he might be allowed to share the delights of the children's tea. He looked round upon them all with eyes in which there were regrets (for he was that strange thing a clergyman without any children of his own), and at the same time that wonder, which is so general with the spectators of such a sight, how it was that they could be happy on so little, and how the parents could look so lighthearted with such a burden on their shoulders—ten children, and the eldest sixteen to-day!

"It is very appropriate that it should be Miss Hetty's little fête," said Mr. Rossmore, "for it is to her, or at least to you about her, that my visit really is intended."

"To Hetty!" her mother cried, with a voice which was half astonishment and half dismay, Mr. Rossmore was a widower, and the horrible thought crossed Mary's mind, Could he have fallen in love with the child? could he mean to propose to her? Awful thought! A man of fifty! She looked at him with alarmed eyes.

"For Hetty?" said Mr. Asquith tranquilly. He thought of parish work, of schools, or some of the minor charities, in which the Vicar might wish Hetty to take a part. And the children, feeling in the midst of their rejoicings that something grave had suddenly come in, looked up with round eyes. Janey edged to the end of the table to listen; for whatever was going on, Janey was always determined to know.

"Perhaps," said Mary tremulously, "it would be better to bring Mr. Rossmore his cup of tea to the drawing-room, now that he has seen you all in the midst of your revels. For this noise is enough to make any one deaf who is not used to it, like papa and me."

69

CHAPTER XIII

A CONFERENCE

THEY all sat down solemnly upon the old chairs, in their faded paint and gilding, with their old seats in fine embroidered work, which had been so handsome in their day, and still breathed of grandparents and an ancestral home. The Asquiths' drawing-room had always been rather heterogeneous, with some things in it which money could not buy, and which they thought very little of, and some that were to be had cheap anywhere, for which, having acquired them by the sweat of their brow, they cared a great deal. They did not remark these contrarieties, having so many other things to think of, but Mr. Rossmore did, and wondered how certain articles came to be there, sometimes asking himself how people with so many graceful old things about them could endure the vulgar new, sometimes what right the purchasers of the vulgar new could have to that beautiful old. He did not know anything about their history, but only that they had a very large family of nice children, and were in consequence poor. They did not themselves say much of their poverty, but the people about did, the chief people in the parish, and especially the district ladies, who were disturbed by it, and wondered, not inaudibly, whether it was possible for the poor Asquiths to give so many children enough to eat. It was this inquiry, very much urged upon him, that had brought Mr. Rossmore here to-day.

He was seized with a little timidity when he began to speak. Something in Mary's look, he could not have told what, an air of dignity, a half-alarm lest something should be said to her which should be unpalatable or offensive, caught and startled him. He could see that the poor incumbent's wife was afraid of being affronted or put in an uncomfortable position by what he was about to say: and in the little gleam of light that thus seemed to fall upon her, Mr. Rossmore began to perceive something more in Mrs. Asquith than the mere parson's wife, with a large family, accustomed to all the shifts of poverty. He became in his turn a little alarmed and nervous, wondering if he should offend them, wondering if——. But he reflected that no reasonable person could have any right to be offended with such a proposal as that he was about to make, and further, that if the Asquiths preferred their pride to the real interests of their children, it was a very poor sort of pride, and not one to be respected. He took courage accordingly, and cleared his throat.

"I hope you will not think what I am going to say impertinent, Mrs. Asquith. I hope I may not be making a mistake. If I am, I am sure I may throw myself on your charity to forgive me—for I mean anything but offence."

"Offence!" said Mr. Asquith. "I am certain of that: and my wife is not a touchy person to take offence."

"I will tell you what it is without more ado," Mr. Rossmore said. "I don't know the people myself, but my brother, who has had to do with the lady in the way of business, has written to me about it. I may be making a mistake," he repeated. "Perhaps you have no such intentions for your children. Miss Hetty perhaps——. But I must tell you what it is. Mrs. Asquith"—he faced towards Mary, for it was of her that he was afraid—"there is a young lady wanted to be with a child in the country—oh, not as a governess: dear me, no, not the least in the world as a governess. This is what it is. There is a little girl in the country, a great heiress, I believe, a little delicate—not queer—no, I don't think she is at all queer. She has a governess with her, an excellent person, very accomplished, a good musician, and speaking all the languages. What they want is a young lady a little older, but not too old to be a companion to the child, who would share all her lessons, and get every advantage, and a salary besides of fifty pounds a year. It is quite an unusual offer, quite a prize for any one who could accept it. I hope, Mrs. Asquith, that you will not think I am taking too much upon me. I thought if you ever contemplated—if, in short, you had thought of—of school or finishing lessons or anything of that sort——"

"Why should you apologise? You are making us the kindest offer. Mary, surely you must feel with me that Mr. Rossmore——"

"I am sure you are very kind," cried Mary, "oh, very kind; nothing could be more kind." There was a little confusion about her, as if she had received a blow: and she was flushed and uneasy. It was something of a shock. To think of Hetty going—to a situation: going—to be somebody's companion! It gave Mary a little sick shock at her heart. But she was a sensible woman, and she had not come thus far on the path of life without learning that pride was a thing to be put at once under the foot of the mother of a family. She regained after a moment entire possession of herself. "It is a little startling to think of Hetty, such a child as she is, going away, earning money," she said, with a quiver of a smile. "It seems so strange, for a girl too. And to lose her out of the house will be something, something——. But, Mr. Rossmore, you are very, very

71

kind. I take it as the greatest kindness. It sounds as if it might be—the very thing for Hetty. Harry, don't you think——"

What with the sudden shock and all the complications of feeling involved, Mrs. Asquith had hard ado not to cry. She laughed a little instead, and looked towards her husband. It was the first time it had ever been suggested to her that her children were not to be always at her side. Mr. Asquith divined a good deal, but not all, that was in her mind.

"My dear," he said, "you are the only person to decide such a matter. Nobody ever understands a girl like her mother. You were anxious about her music, and that she should learn something. To me it seems a wonderful chance, but it is you who must be the judge. Hetty," he said, turning to his brother clergyman with a smile, "is part of herself."

"I can well imagine that; one can see what she is; that is why I came here at once, for if it does not shock you to think of a separation at all, it is a wonderful chance. I never heard in my experience of anything better. The little girl is only ten, but very forward for her age; and Miss Hetty is so used to children."

"And to get all we want for her, and be paid into the bargain;" cried Mary, with a nervous laugh. "We are very much obliged to you, Mr. Rossmore. I am sure Hetty will not hesitate for a moment; and neither do I."

"And where is this wonderful child?" said Mr. Asquith, "and why is she in want of a companion? and where does she live?"

"I don't know the whole story. My brother is in the law. All sorts of romances seem to come into his hands. So far as I can make out, both parents are living, the father mad, shut up in a lunatic asylum; the mother, who has all the money, is abroad. I fancy she's an American, smitten with the love of an old family and an old house."

"It is an old family, then, and an old house."

"They say, one of the most perfect specimens of an old English house, a long way off, though—in Redcornshire—a place called Horton."

Mary uttered a cry. She had thought somehow, she could not tell how, that this name was coming. Mr. Asquith, too, cried, "Horton!" with the wildest amazement, for no presentiment had visited his breast.

"You know the place?" their visitor said.

Mary gave her husband a warning look.

"We knew it very well in our youth, oh, very well. It is startling to hear of it so suddenly. And what is the name of the people who are there now? It is long, long since I have heard."

"Their name is Rotherham," said Mr. Rossmore.

Mary gave her husband once more a look—of mingled relief and disappointment. And then it was decided that Hetty should be called in to hear what she thought of it, and then that Mr. Rossmore should write to his brother the lawyer to say that the wished-for girl had been found. It was all over so quickly, before any one could realise what had taken place. Hetty on being questioned had looked at her mother, and said, "If you can do without me, mamma," with a flush of sudden excitement. She had not hesitated or expressed any alarm. For even Hetty was not impervious to that charm of novelty which is so delightful to youth. There rushed into her young soul all at once a desire to go out to these fresh fields and pastures new, to see the world, to judge for herself what life was like; and then there was the delightful thought that to her, Hetty, only a girl, whom nobody had thought of in that light, should come the privilege—to her the first of all the family—of earning money, of helping at home. Hetty's dreams had taken that shape almost from her childhood, though she had never known how they were to be carried out. Her little romance had been to pay all the bills secretly, so that mamma, when she set out on that hard task of apportioning so much to each, should find, to her amazement, that all had been settled! She had told this dream to Janey, and the two had discussed it often, but never had hit upon a way in which it could be done. Hetty had thought she might perhaps have done it by writing stories, but her first attempt in that way had not been a success. And the girls had generally ended by dwelling on mamma's wonder and joy when she found all the bills paid, and the unusual happiness that would succeed of having a little money and nothing to do with it, and being able to buy a hundred things which at present they had to do without. But now fifty pounds a year! Hetty, it must be allowed, did not take "the advantages" upon which Mr. Rossmore had laid so much stress, and which had been her mother's inducement, much into account. She was not enthusiastic about the lessons. To play the piano better would be pleasant, but it was evident she was not a musician born, for she was without enthusiasm even about that. What she did think of was the glory of being able to help and the pleasure of the novelty: a sensation intensified by feeling, by the thrill of going out into the world like a girl in a novel, and tempered by a sinking of heart which would come upon her when she thought of going away. But at sixteen it is quite possible to get the good of the anticipated novelty and the sensation of going out upon the world, and yet forget the preliminary step, which notwithstanding is of the first necessity, of going away.

The arrangements were not long of being completed. It appeared that little Miss Rotherham lived something of a cloistered life in the great old house. Her mother was away at the other end of the world, and had business or something else to enforce her absence for a year or more, during which time her little girl was under very close regulations. She was not to go outside of the park, except now and then for a drive. She was never to be left alone. If Miss Hofland, the governess, was off duty, her young companion was to be with her, and no visitors or any communication from without were to be allowed. "Extraordinary precautions to be adopted for a child of ten," Mr. Rossmore said. "My brother says there are sufficient family reasons, but does not explain. Except this mystery, I don't know that there is anything to find fault with. The mother is an American. I don't know that this fact affords any explanation. Still their manners are a little different from ours."

"Not in the way of shutting up their children," said Mr. Asquith thoughtfully.

Said Mary, "These regulations don't trouble me. A child of ten is best at home. There is plenty of room for her to walk and play in the park, oh, plenty. You remember, Harry——" There is no telling what recollections might have been called up had not Mr. Rossmore's presence checked them. She paused a little, musing, excited, seeing before her every glade and hollow. "Perhaps the lady is a woman with a system," she said. "She may have some plan of her own for making children perfect. I wonder if Mr. Rossmore knows, Harry—if he knows whether she is related to the old family?"

Mary did not know why it was that she made this inquiry timidly through her husband, as it were at secondhand, instead of inquiring simply as otherwise she should have done. Mr. Rossmore could give no answer to the question. He knew nothing about the Prescotts. And it was so long since they had heard anything, and so much may happen in a dozen years. She said nothing of her relationship, nor that it was her home to which the child was thus going as a stranger. If all were strangers there now, what did it matter? To think that the family had thus disappeared out of Horton gave her a pang. Rotherham? She had never once heard the name before. They must be entirely strangers, foreigners, not even belonging to the neighbourhood. Since the old race had died away, perhaps it was better that it should be so. And it was just as well for Hetty that, since she was going to Horton, she should be kept in this almost monastic seclusion. For Asquith is not a common name, and people might inquire and insist on

74

knowing who Miss Asquith was. It was better, certainly better, that Hetty should not run the risk of cross-examination from old friends. All things were for the best. And, after all, it was only for a year.

Only for a year! While it was a month off, Hetty thought a year nothing at all. She was even conscious of a thrill of eagerness to meet it, a desire to hurry on the time. A year in a romantic old house, in a sort of mediæval retirement, shut in like a princess in a fairy tale! She almost longed to feel the solitude encircle her, the wind blowing among the trees, which was the only sound she should hear. But as the time of her departure approached, Hetty began to change her mind, and the time of her absence to draw out and become larger and larger, till it took the proportions of a century. "They will be quite grown up before I come home," she said to Mary, bending over the curly heads of the two youngest, as they lay in their little cribs side by side: and it took all Hetty's power of self-control to prevent her from bedewing the pillows with her tears. Janey said all she could to comfort the exile. "I wish it was me," Janey cried, whose eyes were dancing with eagerness. "Oh, I wish it was me!" The one dreadful thing, however, which made even Janey acknowledge a pang, was that in four months it would be Christmas, and Hetty would not be able to come home. What kind of Christmas could be possible without Hetty? and oh, what would Hetty do alone, with nobody but a strange little girl of ten and a governess, all by herself on Christmas Day?

CHAPTER XIV

GOING AWAY

"YOU will be sure to write regularly, Hetty, twice a week at the least? You must not forget; you must never forget."

"Oh, never, mamma!" cried poor Hetty, with a quiver in her voice.

"And try if you can hear something about Cousin John. The clergyman is sure to know. Don't ask right out, but try what you can discover. You can say that your mother knew that part of the country, and that you had heard of the Prescotts. Oh, how careless it was of me not to keep on writing! You must be very regular, Hetty—twice a week, at the very least."

"I shall not forget, mamma."

Hetty's poor little face was very pale; her lips were trembling. The family had come, all but the very little ones, to the railway to see her off. But the boys were amused with the locomotive, and the girls with looking at the people; and Hetty felt herself forgotten already. What would it be when she was really away?

And then she relapsed into a spasm of weeping when the inevitable moment came, and the train got into motion. Poor little Hetty! They would all go back, go home, and the business of every day would go on as before, while she was flying away into the unknown, with that clang and wild tumult of sound. Hetty thought she had never realised what a railway journey was before, the clang as of giants' hoofs going, the rush and sweep through the air, as if impelled by some horrible force that could not be appealed to to stop, or made to understand that you wanted to get out, to get out and go back again! This was the first thought of her little scared soul. Horses with a man driving could be made to stop, but this engine never: and what if it should go on, on, to the end of the world? It seemed so likely, so probable that it might do so, in the first dreadful sense of the unescapable which overwhelmed the girl's mind. Of course when she came to herself she was a quite reasonable little girl, and knew that this could not be so, and that, as exactly as is in human possibility, the train would arrive at Horton station, where she was bound, after stopping at many other stations on the way. And presently Hetty dried her eyes, and began to look at the country; and things went a little better with her, until she had another fit of panic and horror at the end of her

76

journey, when she stepped out, trembling, all alone, and saw, half with terror, half with pride, the brougham waiting which was to carry her, behind two sleek and shining horses, in all the glory of a "private carriage" (a thing Hetty knew nothing of), to Horton. She had been driven to the station, she was aware, in the Horton carriage when she went away, a baby, with her parents, and this knowledge—for it was not a recollection—made everything seem all the stranger. It was her mother's home she was going to, and yet such a strange, unknown place.

It seemed to Hetty as if she had known it all her life when the old house came into view. The two wings were a story lower than the centre of the house, which rose into a high roof, with mansard windows rising over the stone parapet; from the east wing the ground sloped away, leaving a rather steep bank of velvet lawn; the other was level with the flower-garden, and seemed partially inhabited. But the lower windows on the west side were all blank and closely shuttered. That was the picture-gallery, Hetty knew, raising its row of long windows above. She wondered if it still was as mamma had so often described it, with the Prescotts' pictures all stately on the walls, her own ancestors, Hetty's ancestors, though nobody knew. The carriage drove up to the door, which did not stand open now, as it had done in mamma's time; only a large person, in a black silk gown, came out, with a not very amiable look, to receive Hetty. "Oh, it's only the young lady," she said, with a slight toss of her head, and bade an attendant maid look after the little box and bag which contained the girl's modest requirements. Then, with a wave of her hand, this grand personage bade Hetty follow, and led her through the hall and a long passage to a bright room behind, looking out upon the trimmest of artificial gardens, all cut out in flower-beds, and still blazing with colour, red geraniums and yellow calceolarias and asters in all colours, though it was October. The colour and the light almost dazzled Hetty, after the cool, subdued tones of the hall. Here a little girl, with her hair in a flood over her shoulders— dark hair, very much crêpé—sat at the piano, with a tall and slim figure, on which from top to toe the word "governess" seemed written, seated beside her. The child went on playing like a little automaton; but the lady rose when Hetty came timidly in, following the housekeeper. "Here's the young lady, Miss Hofland," that personage said, with little ceremony, and turned away without another word. Miss Hofland was very thin, very gentle, with a slightly deprecating air. She put out her hand to Hetty, and gave her an emphatic grasp, which seemed to mean an exhortation to silence as well as a greeting. "How do you do? Rhoda's at her lesson," she said in a half-whisper, signing to the girl to sit down, which Hetty, breathless with the oppressive sense of novelty and strangeness, was very glad to do. She sat down feeling as if she had fallen out of a different planet, out of another world, while the little girl went on playing her exercises, with the "One, two, three, four, one, two, three, four," of the governess's half-whispering voice. What a curious scene it was! Hetty had time to note everything in the room, and to take in the red and yellow and blue of the flower-beds outside, and the pictures on the walls, and the trifles on the table, while the stumbling sound of the piano, now checked to have a passage played over again, now pounding monotonously with that "One, two, three," went on and on. Little Miss Rotherham's hair was very dark, very much crimped, and standing out in a bush, very unlike the natural fair locks of the children at home. She was about the same size as little Mary, Hetty said to herself, but Mary played better, though she had never had any lessons, and her hair was so soft, falling with just a soft twist in it, which was natural. But oh, how much happier Mary must be with all her brothers and sisters. Hetty ended by saying, "Poor little thing!" to herself quite softly as the lesson went on.

When Rhoda got up from her lesson, she came, instructed by the governess, and gave Hetty her hand, and said, "How do you do, Miss Asquith?" She had a little dark face, quite in keeping with her dark hair, and a small person, very slight and straight, not round and plump, as the Asquiths were at that age. Hetty, who, by reason of her large family was truly maternal in her way, and knew all about children, regretted instinctively that this little thing was so thin, and wondered if she were delicate, or if she were getting better of something, which might account for it. At the same moment a footman brought in tea—a footman in livery, who seemed to Hetty's unaccustomed eyes grotesque and out of place—and then the three proceeded to make acquaintance over their bread-and-butter.

"You have had rather a long journey. I fear you must be very tired," the governess said.

"Oh no," said Hetty. "It is not like walking. In the railway there is nothing to tire one."

"Don't you think so? But perhaps you have had a great deal of travelling?"

"I never," said Hetty, the tears coming to her eyes, "was away from home before."

"That is always rather a trial," said Miss Hofland, sympathetically, "but I hope you'll soon feel quite at home with Rhoda and me. We are all that is here, nothing but Rhoda and me,

78

and the servants of course. We lead a very quiet life, but you heard of that, no doubt. We take our walk in the park, and we pay great attention to our lessons, oh, great attention, Miss Asquith. We are working very hard in order to astonish mamma when she comes back. We think that when she sees the progress that has been made, she will be very much pleased."

At this Rhoda lifted up a somewhat sharp little voice, and declared that she did not think mamma cared.

"Oh, how can you say so, my dear child? No one knows how much mothers care. Perhaps they may not say so to their little girls, but it is the first wish of their hearts to see their children get on. Isn't that so, Miss Asquith? I am sure you know."

"It is mamma's first wish—oh, to have everything she can for the children," cried Hetty, the tears, which were so very near her eyes, coming again.

"I told you so, Rhoda," said Miss Hofland, with a little air of triumph.

Rhoda made no reply. Her soul apparently was filled with no thought but bread-and-butter. There was a precocious gravity and stiffness about her which half frightened Hetty. It appeared that it was Miss Hofland who was the nearest her own age, while Rhoda was years beyond them both in seriousness, learned in all the cares of earth. This impression did not diminish for the first week of Hetty's sojourn at Horton. Familiarity dispelled it a little afterwards, and made her perceive that the child's gravity was one of the many marks of shyness, and that the nature beneath was, after all, like child-nature in general, thoughtless and changeable, varying to natural gaiety when the sense of strangeness was overcome. But still there was a shadow upon the little face which not even shyness could account for. This was partly physical, for the little girl had immense dark eyes, with long eyelashes, which overshadowed her little countenance, and partly mental, as if some cloud hung over her, unknown to the rest of the world. It was not till Hetty had grown familiar with the strange secluded life of the place that she knew anything more. It was a very strange life, the house full of servants, the imperious housekeeper managing everything as if no one but herself had to be consulted, and the three simple feminine creatures for whom, so far as appeared, all this costly household existed, living in their little spot of space— the morning room, which opened on the garden; the spare, nicely furnished place in which they dined; the set of bedrooms on the same side of the house—all these rooms were on the ground floor, one opening into another. Between Hetty's room and that of Miss Hofland ran a passage, but this was the only division. Rhoda's maid slept in the room beyond Hetty's. They were thus altogether separated from the rest of the house. And so far as the bright tints of a cheerful garden could give animation, everything in their outlook was bright. Their sitting-room communicated with a conservatory. They had flowers in abundance, an aviary of birds among the flowers, and everything sweet and graceful about them. They were like princesses living in an enchanted garden, their little meals exquisitely cooked and served by the same magnificent man in livery, wonderful hothouse fruits always produced for their dessert. To Hetty the wealth seemed boundless that surrounded her. Was this, she wondered, how country houses were always kept up? Mamma had said the Prescotts were poor. To be sure, the Prescotts were here no longer. "But what a change," she said to herself, "what a wonderful change for mamma, from Horton to that little house at home, overflowing with children. Oh, what a change!" Hetty did not remember that the children had come by degrees, and that gradually the sphere of existence and all its motives had changed for Mary. The wide greenness of the park, the giant trees, the pushing aside, as it were, of the world, so that breathing space and quiet might be secured for those favourites of fortune, produced a great effect upon Hetty. And to think that her mother had been brought up amid those shady glades and wide stretches of tranquil greenness! "Oh," thought Hetty, "what would she give only to have permission to walk in such a park with the children now?"

When she had become quite familiar with this strange life, and had begun to feel herself, as people say, "at home," although it was so different, so very different, so much worse and better than home, Hetty acquired various scraps of information about the strange household. There were never any visitors at Horton except the doctor and the clergyman, the former a young man, very grave and sedate in appearance, who appeared frequently at the house, and was constantly met by the little party in their walks in the park, when he seemed to be going or coming from the Hall, but always stopped to explain that he was on his way to some distant place, and had taken advantage of the permission he had to take the short cut across the park. The clergyman, on the other hand, was old and very cheerful, a gay little white-haired old man, who took tea about once a week with Miss Hofland and her charges, and whose visits were their brightest moments, Mr. Hayman, the rector, was always gay; the young doctor, whose name was Darrell, was always serious. Except these two, nobody ever came to the house. This roused little questions in the mind of Hetty, who was young enough to accept whatever happened as the common order of affairs. And it was only when Miss Hofland took the girl into her confidence that any question arose in her mind. Miss Hofland was older and more alive to the peculiarities of their cloistered life.

"Don't you think it is a strange thing, my dear," she said to Hetty suddenly, when she had been about a month at Horton, "that a mother should go away to the end of the world for a whole year, and leave her only little child all alone in a big house like this?"

They had been sitting together over the fire for a long time in silence. Rhoda had gone to bed, the great silence of the wintry park had closed over the house, and there was the darkness of a moonless night, which seemed somehow to creep into the rooms, and intensify the stillness and sense of seclusion from all the world. Hetty was much startled by this question. It took her some time to think what her companion could mean—a mother at the end of the world, and an only little child all alone! She looked up surprised, repeating almost unconsciously, "A mother—at the end of the world!"

"Yes," said Miss Hofland; "don't say you haven't asked yourself the same——"

"Do you mean—Rhoda?" faltered Hetty, feeling as if the suggestion was in some sort a betrayal of trust.

"I mean Rhoda's mother; who else could I mean? Did you ever hear of such a thing before? There are a great many things I don't understand about this house."

Hetty gazed once more, but put no answering question, nothing that could induce the governess to go on. The girl's fine sense of good faith was shocked. It seemed to be a sort of wickedness and treachery to discuss the circumstances of the place in which she was living. But all the same these questions liberated Hetty's own thoughts. Now that it had been suggested to her, she too became aware of many wonderings on the eve of bursting forth. Why? and why? But there was no answer to be had.

81

CHAPTER XV

FIRESIDE TALK

"I HAVE been here only six months," said Miss Hofland. "I am engaged for a year, like you. I was sent on trial at first to see if the child would take to me, poor little thing! I didn't think she could take to anybody: but I've changed my opinion." She added, "Hetty, she is fond of you."

"Poor child!"

"Yes, poor child! but she is a rich child at the same time, and luckier a great deal than either you or I."

"Oh, don't say so, Miss Hofland. If you had ever been with us at home, you would not say any one was happier than me."

"Well, my dear, so much the better for you. I never pretended to be very happy. I have no home at all, and I have been teaching children in one house and another since I was sixteen. I have never had any youth. It is hard to go on teaching all one's life, and that not even for somebody one cares for, but only just for one's self, to keep the life in one, which one doesn't much wish to keep."

"Oh, Miss Hofland!" Hetty cried.

"It is quite true, my dear. Why should one? One has to live, because one has been brought into the world. And then one goes on working, a stranger everywhere, never with any home just in order to have enough to eat and clothes to put on. Oh, I have always envied the poor girls, whom everybody is sorry for, who have to send their money home to their mothers! It has always been said I was so well off, I had nobody but myself to think of. Well, don't let us talk like this. It frightens you, and it does me no good. My dear, this is a very strange house."

"It is very quiet," Hetty hazarded: and then felt frightened for what she had said.

"Quiet! It wasn't quiet at one time, I believe, when she first married him; and now they say he's mad, and she is away. And why is that doctor always about, my dear? Don't you notice how often he is here? The servants are not always ill, but my belief is that Mr. Darrell is here every day; and when we meet him in the park, how is it that he's always so anxious to explain where he's going? I don't understand about that man."

"He looks very nice," said Hetty, apologetically, feeling that it was hard to condemn a man who probably was not to blame.

"Oh, he is nice enough. I don't say anything about his niceness. But why is he so often here? Mrs. Mills is not a confirmed invalid, but he is always having long talks with her, and when any one sees them they look startled. Would you like to hear what I think? I think both Mrs. Mills and Mr. Darrell are in the secret, and know why Mrs. Rotherham is away: and perhaps Mr. Hayman too."

"But then it must be quite right if the clergyman knows it," said Hetty, brought up with a faith in clergymen which her companion did not share. Miss Hofland shook her head.

"I don't say it's right, and I don't say it's wrong. I say it's very strange. Clergymen know very queer things sometimes. They can't help it. Indeed, people who do queer things are very apt in my experience to tell a clergyman. It seems like getting a sanction to it. If he tells them not to do it, they don't mind; they take their own way: but they always feel a satisfaction in thinking he knows. It shares the responsibility. He can't be so very hard upon them after if he has known all the time: and I daresay some of them think they can persuade God it's all right, because the clergyman knows."

"Oh, Miss Hofland!" cried Hetty again.

"My dear, I know you are shocked by what I say; and I wouldn't speak to you in this way if I had any one else to speak to. It is more than human nature is equal to, to keep quite silent. One can't help noticing, you know. I've been in a great many houses, and known a great many family secrets. There is almost always something to find out, but generally it is quite on the surface; either it is a son who is making them unhappy, or a girl who has a love affair, or husband and wife don't get on: these are the common things. But this place is full of mystery. Don't you feel it in the air?"

"I should never have thought of anything——" said Hetty: and paused, afraid to seem to reproach her companion, or to say anything that was not quite true.

"If I had not put it in your head? I shouldn't wonder. When I was like you, I never took any notice. You are not what I call governessy, my dear: but you would be the same as I am if you went in for my kind of life. I can't help noticing now. I find out things without meaning to; you do when you are in a family without belonging to it, and have no occupation for your mind but to watch, and nobody to say it to. Then every little thing is an interest, and to put two and two together—— But I won't frighten you. Do your people intend you to be a governess, my dear?"

This question gave Hetty a still greater shock than all the

83

rest. She cried, "Oh, I hope not!" in instinctive alarm; then grew very red, and looked wistfully at her companion, feeling that to repudiate Miss Holland's profession in this eager way might be an offence.

"You would always have your family to fall back upon," said Miss Hofland, "and you would be able to help them. If there are so many of you, it would be your duty to do that. And though it's not Paradise, it's better than marrying a poor curate, and bringing dozens of children into the world to misery, which is probably what you would do if you were not a governess. I am not fond of this way of living, but it's better than that; at least you have nobody but yourself, and when you die there's an end of it. The first money I ever laid by was just enough to bury me. I've always kept that safe. I should like to have things decent, and not to be thrown on charity for my last expenses. And when that comes, there's an end of it: that's a great comfort; nobody else will be left to trouble and toil on account of me."

The governess delivered this little monologue in quite a cheerful tone of voice, without any appearance of being deeply moved by it; her dismal philosophy was so unaffected that it had ceased to touch her feeling. She described this desolate mental condition in tones of steady matter of fact, while the young creature beside her gazed at her with a dismay which was speechless. A thousand thoughts ran through Hetty's mind as she spoke. To be a governess! would not that be her duty? ought not that to be her life too? She had never been called on to think of such questions. There was so much to do at home. It had not occurred to her that she could even be spared. To help mamma seemed the natural use of the eldest girl. Now there swept through Hetty's mind a tumult of confused thoughts and newly-awakened alarms. Ah! who could doubt it? This was what must, what ought to be, that she who was the eldest should go out into the world and help the rest. How often had she heard mamma wondering, calculating how to get the boys the needful indispensable education, which would be necessary to fit them for making their way; and it had never occurred to Hetty to say, "Of course I must go and be a governess, and send home the money." Was it perhaps because she did not know enough to teach? But she knew enough for the nursery. She did teach the little ones at home. And now another thought suddenly leaped into her young soul. Her mother had sent her because of the "advantages," advantages to which Hetty had given so little thought. She perceived it all now. This was why mamma wanted her to have advantages, that she might be fitted for the life she would have to adopt, that she might be clever enough to be a governess! The discovery (as she thought it) fell into Hetty's little heart like lead, and then a flush of shame swept over her—that she should not have divined it for herself; that she should not have seen that as the eldest it was her duty to help, and to help steadily. This was quite different from the little romance of paying the bills secretly, which had so much delighted her imagination; as much different as the actual burden of life is from the enthusiasm of the ideal. It did not inspire her as that had done; on the contrary, it fell upon her like something crushing and terrible. Not for this year only, as she had thought—not to go back triumphant with her fifty pounds, and buy mamma a sealskin, and settle forever at home. Ah, no! very different. She had left home for good, Hetty said to herself; she must never think of home again but as a holiday refuge. Her destiny was like Miss Hofland's—to live in other people's houses, to teach other people's children, to lay up carefully out of her first earnings enough to bury her. Oh, dreadful, dreadful thought! All this while Miss Hofland went on quietly with her talk, not distressed at all by the miserable provision which she had thought it right to make.

"You should get up a little earlier to practise, my dear. I shall always be willing to give you a little more time. Rhoda could do very well without you for an hour in the afternoon, after dinner, you know. And if you liked to take up any subject after she has gone to bed?—We might read a little French, for instance; or German. You don't know German at all, do you? I never grudge a little trouble when it's for a purpose, and to help on one who has an object. One has more satisfaction in doing that—helping a comrade, as the men would say—than giving lessons to a pack of little girls who don't want to learn, and never will do any good with it. Should you like to begin German? Well, my dear, I'll look you out my old grammars, and we'll begin to-morrow night."

"You are very, very kind, Miss Hofland. What can I ever do for you, to show my gratitude? Mamma will be so thankful: so—happy."

It went against the grain with Hetty in the first pang of this discovery to think that mamma would be happy, and yet there was nothing but thanks and gratitude due to Miss Hofland. The girl was half choked by this conflict of gratitude and misery, and did not know what to say.

"Well, my dear, you must work very hard, and take advantage of all your opportunities," said Miss Hofland; "one always regrets it in after life if one misses a chance. But it's time now to go to bed. One wise thing in this hermitage," she added, "is that they give us such good fires. Is your fire always good, my

85

dear?" The governess followed Hetty along the corridor, into which this suite of rooms opened. It was very dimly lighted, and the two figures with their twinkling candles had a mysterious effect between the two dark wainscoted walls, which reflected the flicker of the lights. Miss Hofland went with Hetty into her room, and looked round it. "Yours is the only French window," she said; "it opens into the garden, don't you know. I prefer the sash-windows, they are much safer. But why don't they shut your shutters and draw your curtains, my dear? You must not put up with any neglect."

"Oh, I don't like it so dark. I like to see the sky. I can't breathe when the curtains are drawn. I am not accustomed to curtains," said Hetty, feeling that she was making a confession of poverty. Miss Hofland gave an approving nod.

"It is a great deal better for the health," she said; "still I can't sleep unless it is dark, and they keep out the cold in this big house. I hope you always see that your window is well fastened. I must speak to Mrs. Mills about it. To live in this queer way, with a regiment of servants and not to be attended to, would be too absurd. Good-night, my dear," Miss Hofland said. Her room was on the other side of the little passage, which also had a window looking out across the flower-beds of the parterre to the ghostly depths of the park. It was a moonlight night, and they both lingered looking out upon the strange, silent scene. The flower-beds were full of winterly chrysanthemums—for it was by this time November—which drooped their tall heads in the frosty air. The trees beyond stood up half stripped, showing here and there their great branches, with a leaf or two fluttering in the wind against the sky. Miss Hofland opened her own door with a shudder. "How cold it looks," she said—"how still and deserted! I am glad everything is snug and shut up in my room. If I were to look out much longer I should see ghosts, I know I should. Run away, my dear, and get to bed."

Hetty heard the little click of the key which Miss Hofland always turned at night, a precaution which had amused the girl on her first coming. "Fancy mamma locking her door!" she had said to herself. But it was eerie standing by that passage window by herself. She went back to her room and put down her candle, and took down her hair. Her mother had always been proud of Hetty's hair. It was brown and silky, and very abundant, and, indeed, it was not so very long since it was first twisted up in that grown-up way which had made Hetty feel so dignified. Now that she had attained to that privilege she liked to shake it down, and feel it about her, rippling over her shoulders. But she had no leisure for any play that night. Her mind was overwhelmed with her new thoughts. An entire revelation had been made to her of her duty, of what girls were born for. To think she should have been so stupid, to suppose that all that was wanted was helping mamma with the children, mending, making, overlooking the housework! No, indeed, that was not all. It would be years before even Harry, the eldest boy, could earn anything; while Hetty was the eldest of all, and the first claim of duty naturally came to her. She strayed towards the window, half-undressed, to look out as people naturally do when they are full of thought, without any regard even to the moonlight, not thinking of anything outside, absorbed in those meditations which were not cheerful. The long pale distance between the trees, the masses of distant shadow, the chrysanthemums drooping as if whispering to each other close at hand, seemed to give a little air and outlet to the musing of her heart.

But all at once Hetty gave a smothered cry, and clung to the nearest solid thing, feeling as if the ground was reeling away from under her feet. Over the grass, which was damp and sodden with winter dews, winding among the beds and ranks of chrysanthemums, what was that she saw? Something black in the moonlight, a moving figure, the sight of which made her heart stand still. Her eyes seemed to strain out of her head, her heart to jump into her throat in sudden panic and horror. A man! Hetty rushed to the door in the first impulse after her senses returned to her; but then she remembered the key turned in Miss Hofland's door; and though she opened her own softly, she closed it again, and locked it too, in her terror. And then she returned to the window, drawn as by a spell, to watch that mysterious figure slowly moving round and round among the drooping winter flowers.

CHAPTER XVI

ALARMS

"HAVE you a headache, my dear? I am sure you have a headache. You are looking quite ghostly. Poor little thing! you look as if you had not slept all night."

"Oh, it is nothing," said Hetty. "I didn't sleep very well, I got off my sleep somehow."

"I know; people talk about the sleep of youth, but I can remember many nights, when I was a girl like you, when I never closed my eyes. Take your tea, my dear, and it will refresh you. I suppose as you couldn't sleep you got to thinking, and cried for your mother like a baby, and to go home."

"Oh, Miss Hofland!" cried Hetty.

"Yes, I know very well how girls do who have got mothers to cry after. I used to envy them, not having one. Don't cry now, but take your breakfast and cheer up a little. Have a little of this nice toast. When you cannot have what you want, you should try to get all the good you can out of what you have," the governess said. This philosophy of her profession was dreary, and not suited to Hetty's tremulous and unaccustomed ease.

"Didn't you sleep?" said Rhoda. "Oh, isn't it awfully quiet in the night when one can't sleep?" The child, who had thawed very much out of her first gravity, threw her arms round Hetty and kissed her; but while she gave her this embrace asked, with a nervous whisper in her ear, "Did you hear anything?—did you see anything?" with an anxious look.

"I heard the stable clock, and the hours striking from the village," said Hetty. "Oh! don't say anything more. It was only that I cou'dn't sleep."

Mrs. Mills looked keenly at her from the other side of the table. She seemed to examine the girl's pale face with questioning eyes. She came in every morning while they were at breakfast, for orders, she said, but there were never any orders to give her. She suggested what there was to be for dinner, if the ladies pleased; and the ladies generally did please, though Miss Hofland, to show her independence, would make an alteration now and then.

"It's cheerful to hear the clocks when one can't sleep," said Mrs. Mills, as if it were possible that she could have heard Rhoda's question. "And in this quiet place there is nothing else to hear, unless one was to believe the stories of the ghosts about the place, and there's not much sense in them."

"I beg you won't speak of anything of the kind before Miss Rhoda!" cried the governess, sharply. "And you, Hetty, you're trembling, you silly child!"

"N—no, Miss Hofland," Hetty said; but her head was racked with pain, and she scarcely knew what she said. Was it a ghost she had seen, a disembodied soul? She had not been so entirely without sleep as she thought, but had dozed and woke again, always in a fever of alarm and misery, recalling to herself the long muffled figure, the slow, soft, noiseless movements, the winding out and in of the flower beds where the yellow and brown heads of the chrysanthemums drooped in the frost. It seemed to stand before her now as Mrs. Mills stood—though very unlike Mrs. Mills—a long thin figure, wrapped from head to foot in some clinging garment.

"If I speak it is in a joke," said Mrs. Mills; "you don't think I believe in anything of the sort?"

"I don't admire that kind of joking," Miss Hofland said. "Rhoda, come, if you have finished your breakfast it is quite time to begin lessons. I think we are a little late to-day."

Hetty followed, heavy-eyed and heavy-hearted, her mind oppressed with the secret, which was a burden almost beyond her power of supporting. Should she tell Miss Hofland? she kept asking herself. Should she ask Mrs. Mills? And oh! what was it? it was no thief watching the house, of that Hetty was sure. The fantastic movements of the figure among those flower-beds came up before her eyes a hundred times, and made her almost cry out with terror. She remembered the very poise of the figure, light, with a little swing in the step. Could that be a ghost that moved in such a human way, not gliding, not mystical, as ghosts are described as being? Her head turned round as again and again the moonlight scene rose before her. It seemed impossible to get it out of her eyes. She closed them, to rest her hot strained eyeballs, and lo, there it was before her in those wonderful contrasts of black and white, so clear, so clear! the broad stretch of wistful silvery mist and distance behind, the black solid line of the moving object, the tall flowers drooping their heads, the trees gathering like spectators on every side. The hum of the voices near her was to Hetty's ears like a monotonous murmur without meaning. When it came to her turn to read or answer a question, she raised a white face without intelligence to the governess. "My dear, you have not been attending," Miss Hofland cried, astonished; but this by degrees changed into, "My dear, you must be ill. Is your head bad?

have you caught cold? What is the matter?" Miss Hofland was very philosophical on her own account, but to the young people under her charge she was kind, and it was understood in her code of laws that a headache was always to be respected, being in some sort a girl's only refuge in heartache and all other ills.

"I feel dreadfully stupid," said Hetty, not knowing how to excuse herself.

"It is your head that is bad. You will be better if you will go and lie down," said Miss Hofland; but this was a remedy that made Hetty shiver. Lie down with her face towards the window from which she had seen that sight, or, worse still, turning her back to it, so that the figure might be performing any kind of wild gyration behind her! This made the throbbing in her head and the fluttering at her heart worse than ever.

"Oh no!" she cried, "I don't want to lie down; let me stay here—oh! let me stay with you. It is so much nicer to be with you."

"Then lie down on the sofa," said the governess, "and try to go to sleep. Poor little thing! how you are trembling, your nerves are all wrong. That's what it is to have a nuit blanche when one is young."

"Did you hear anything, Hetty? did you see anything?" cried little Rhoda in her ear, while Miss Hofland covered her up. Hetty, in the agony of her unwonted secret, did not know how to make any reply. She had never known what it was to have a secret before. To know something which she kept to herself seemed wrong to Hetty. If there ever was any little thing unknown to mamma, such as that project for the private paying of the bills, it was breathed to Janey. Little secrets about Christmas presents and suchlike—secrets so little, so innocent—were always shared with somebody. To have this dark knowledge in her heart, and nobody to tell it to, made Hetty's heart sick. And Rhoda's big eyes appealing to her made everything more difficult. She had heard nothing, not a sound, which made what she had seen still more weird and unearthly. And what did the child mean, whispering as if she had a secret too?

Hetty, however, slumbered a little in the warm room, with the protecting sense of society round her, and the hum of the voices in her ears. Nothing could happen there to her that would not be known. If that thing should really appear again, at least Miss Hofland would be there to see it too. This soothed and brought the ease of rest to the feverish brain.

But when night came again, and Hetty had to go to bed by herself in that room, with the window as usual open to the sky, and the formal flower-beds with the chrysanthemums all spread out in the moonlight, and the consciousness that Miss Hofland had turned the key in her door, and shut herself off from all possibility of appeal, Hetty's sensations of alarm were indescribable. She rushed to the window and drew the curtains close that she might not see out; then, feeling still more intolerable the thought that outside, in the whiteness of the moon, that ghastly thing might be pacing, drew them back again in a panic, and gazed out in a trance of speechless terror. But the white light fell unbroken over the garden, and the long vista of the park opened before her, a wistful vacancy stretching to the sky, without a living thing to disturb the scene. Hetty stood clinging to the curtains, half hidden in their folds, as if she were herself afraid to be seen, for a long time, she did not know how long. But there was no movement or shadow upon the undisturbed stillness, and ghostly, motionless, half-frozen calm without. She stood there till she was chilled to the heart with cold; her fire had gone out; her candles were nearly burnt to the socket, and nature began to assert her rights. The stable clock shrilling all the hours close at hand, and the village clock booming in a minute after like a bass accompaniment, were half consoling, half alarming. Twelve! how long it took to strike! and was not this the hour "when churchyards yawn and graves give up——" Hetty hung upon the curtains, half unconscious, for a minute or two; if she had not grasped them so she would have fallen, and probably fainted. But the support of the heavy, thick folds, which sustained her slight little figure, kept her from that climax. And after a time she crept to bed and slept soundly, and woke wondering at herself; trying to laugh at herself; chiding herself for all this excitement. Her night's rest had restored her nerves. She appeared at breakfast, if still a little tremulous, yet herself again, and smiled as she met Miss Hofland's sympathetic inquiries, and Mrs. Mills' keen look. Why did Mrs. Mills look at her with that gaze of suspicion? and little Rhoda, with her big eyes, seizing the first opportunity to whisper, "Did you hear anything?" The look and the question raised again a little flutter in her spirits, but she felt brave in the strength of her night's sleep, and of the passage of time, which has always a soothing effect: and began to forget.

Another night passed, and she saw nothing, and then another day. The girl felt more safe; life began to wear its usual aspect. It might be one of the servants after all; some one, perhaps, who did not venture to go into the garden during the day, and who had heard of the chrysanthemums; or it might be the gardener, stealing out to cover some of his more delicate plants. None of those common-sense explanations had occurred to Hetty at first.

91

They came upon her now in a crowd. Of course she said to herself, How foolish not to have thought of it before! The frosts were beginning to be harder every night; what more natural than that the gardener should take every precaution against the severe weather? In the reaction from her panic, Hetty became more cheerful, more gay than ever. If suddenly her vision came before her eyes and chilled her, she flung it away, saying to herself: how silly! Why was it that she had not seen how easily the thing was to be accounted for before?

This continued for some time. She was not so courageous when she went into her room at night. There she invariably passed half an hour or so enveloped in the curtains, gazing out; but with less and less alarm, sometimes even with a little bravado, opening her window, giving herself the keen and thrilling sensations of the wintry night. And a long time passed before she had any occasion for a renewal of her alarm. It was close upon Christmas when the second incident occurred. Suddenly, in the grey of a rainy night, as she took her accustomed stand, something seemed to move outside, and brought her heart with a leap into her throat. Something moved; that was all. She could distinguish nothing; the grey of the night, the soft haze of the falling rain, filled up the landscape. The opening of the park was but a pale blotch upon the surrounding darkness. After the first moment of pain, Hetty chid herself again. Yes, she said to herself, something moved. Of that there was no doubt; the rain falling down straight through the windless air moved, of course, keeping a sensation of flow and action in the immovable atmosphere. But this did not still the beating of her heart. She pressed close to the window, holding it with her hand, peering out into the grey. To see anything was impossible through the veil of that falling rain. It went on, not violently—softly, a gentle cold stream of imperceptible drops, soaking everything, obliterating sound and sight. Who could see, had they the sharpest eyes in the world, through that mist of continuous dropping? who could hear anything, had they ears as keen as those of a savage? And yet Hetty, with her heart beating so loud that it filled all the world with commotion, both heard and saw and knew that something—she could not tell what—something living, that had a will and action of its own, was somewhere near her outside, disguised and enveloped in the soft pouring of the rain. She said to herself, the gardener, one of the servants, as she had done before; but her heart was sick with terror. She could not satisfy herself with that argument; half the night through she watched; and yet she could not say that she had seen anything. No, nothing at all, nothing at all! but she felt in every fibre, in every nerve, that someone had been there.

This time she resolved on telling Miss Hofland. It was impossible to live under the spell of this terror. She must, at least—she must—have somebody to share it; and insensibly she began to hope that perhaps Miss Hofland, being older, and having seen so much in her life, might be able to suggest some explanation, and clear the mystery up. Hetty slept little that night. Her resolution gave her a little steadiness, but it did not restore her calm; and in the dawn of the winter morning she was up before any one, unable to rest. When there was something like daylight in the grey skies, a ghost of morning just making the garden and its formal flower-beds visible, she stole again to her window; and finally, encouraged by the hour, and the consciousness that, though there was still so little light, it was day and not night that was approaching, opened it softly and stole out. The rain had ceased, but everything was sodden and wet, her foot sinking into the spongy grass, which came close up to the window ledge. There was nothing there that could conceal any lurking figure. If there had been anything, any clandestine visitor, whoever it was must have crouched by the wall, close, close to where she stood within. Hetty thought she saw some of the moss upon the wall scraped away as by some one rubbing against it; and her heart sprang up once more with the flutter of terror to think of this possibility. Only the wall between her—so young, so frightened, and helpless—and that presence, whether spirit or man, whatever it was. It was all she could do to stand upon her trembling limbs and keep upright, though it was now morning and no longer dark. And when suddenly something appeared round the corner of the house, a dark figure making its way towards her, she could not restrain a scream as she flew back to the shelter of her window. Quick as her movements were, she was not quick enough, however, to elude this presence; and Hetty's fear gave place to a stupefied astonishment when she recognised the doctor, Mr. Darrell, who touched her shoulder, and called her by her name.

"Let me speak to you a moment," he said, breathlessly. "I fear I have disturbed you—perhaps more than once."

"You!" was all that Hetty could say, panting with fright, relief, and profound surprise above all. He was in his usual dress, looking somehow as if he had not taken it off all night, and looked harassed and pale.

"Yes," he said. "I was afraid you had seen me, and might be frightened. I have a patient with whom I have to be at all hours, both night and day; who is not quite sane but quite harmless. Forgive me; and might I ask you not to speak of it to frighten the house?"

CHAPTER XVII

SHUTTING UP

TO say nothing of it, to frighten the house! Hetty had never encountered in her own youthful person such a difficulty before. To keep the secret of something which had happened, which now it was very clear to her was not accidental—something perhaps that might be important, to keep the secret from those whom it might concern! In a moment her little fiction about the gardener disappeared, and she felt that she had never truly believed it. Something of far greater meaning lay beneath. She confronted it vaguely with frightened eyes; the conditions of her coming, and of the life here, and of Miss Hofland's wonder and questioning, all flashing upon her in a moment. Everything went to prove that there was a mystery involved, something connected with the family that probably ought not to be concealed. She looked at Mr. Darrell with eyes which woke from a sort of stupefaction of fear and wonder into intelligence and acute anxiety. She did not speak, having scarcely regained sufficient possession of herself to trust her voice, but examined him with those awakened eyes.

"There is nothing wrong," he said, with a slight tremulousness. "I would not deceive you. Whatever may be the rights of the matter, nothing could be gained by disturbing the house."

"Oh, what is it?" cried Hetty, in spite of herself.

He shook his head with a smile. "Nothing," he said, "that can affect you, nothing indeed. You have seen or heard me going to my patient?"

"Oh, Mr. Darrell," said Hetty, with the indignation of sincerity, "it was not you."

He shrank a little from her look. "I think you are mistaken," he said; "how can you tell in the night who it is? I have to be about at all hours. I go through the park, or even across the garden, as the shortest way."

Hetty eyed him once more with the superiority of fact over fiction. She looked at him as if she saw through him, he thought, and, what was worse, undervalued him, and set him down as a deceiver. In reality Hetty was far too much perplexed and disturbed in her mind to come to any such decided conclusion. She was looking at him instinctively to try to make him out. And in this look a great many things were communicated by the one to the other which did not at all involve the immediate question. Hetty saw a face which was full of anxiety, and perhaps of desire to veil a certain secret, but which at the same time was open and true, the countenance of a man in whom guile was not. The true recognise the true, however different may be their mental altitude or position. She thought he was deceiving her, and yet by instinct she believed in him. And he saw, in the young face lifted to him with such troubled questioning, the look of a judge before whose decision he trembled. If she should judge him from the surface, as it was so natural she should—if she took the fiction on his lips for the indication of his character, the young doctor in a moment felt that the work in which he was engaged, and which already his conscience disapproved, would cost him dear.

"Miss Asquith," he said, hurriedly, "I must not stop to explain. Will you remember, whatever may happen, that I am always about? even when you don't see anything of me, I'm near. Don't let yourself be frightened; whatever happens, I am always near."

"It would be better to tell me what it is. Then I could not be frightened," said Hetty, with as much calm as she could muster. But before he could reply, he no less than she started at the sound of a step—one step and no more, at which she clutched his arm with terror unspeakable, and he looked quickly round with a look of alarm in which there was no counterfeit. There was but one step, which was a thing to curdle the blood, as it seemed to Hetty, more than any succession of footsteps—one single stealthy step and no more.

"Who is there? Speak," cried the young doctor, with a voice which was not loud, but seemed to penetrate the intense morning stillness like a knife. And then, while Hetty stood speechless, there suddenly appeared round the corner of the house the paltry figure of Mrs. Mills the housekeeper, in extremely simple morning apparel, with a scared look in her face.

"Oh, Mr. Darrell, is it you?" she cried in her turn, in a voice full of relief.

It would have been embarrassing for an older and more experienced young woman than Hetty to find herself discovered by the housekeeper in close colloquy with young Mr. Darrell, in the early morning before the house was astir. But Hetty was too young for any such feeling. She was frightened, but relieved beyond measure. It is not pleasant to think that even the housekeeper stands and looks in at your window in the grey of the morning before any one is awake. But still this seemed to Hetty, somehow, more possible than if it had been the doctor making mysterious,

95

impossible journeys round the house. Her hand dropped from that clutch upon his arm. She felt restored at once to the practicable world.

"I am trying to persuade Miss Asquith," he said, "that she heard nothing worse than myself passing through the garden, and that she must not be surprised if she hears me again."

The woman, who looked pale, as if she had been up all night, melted into an uneasy smile. "No, no, she mustn't be afraid. There are a many noises about this house," she said.

"Nothing more than the doctor going his rounds, late or early," said Darrell; "you will believe Mrs. Mills? And now go back to your room, and I hope you won't let me disturb your rest again. Remember," he said, with emphasis, "I'm always about. I'm always near."

"You've got your window all open, miss," said the housekeeper. "Bless me! it should always be well fastened and the shutters shut. I must give the housemaid a piece of my mind."

Hetty followed her in, unresisting, as she pushed into the privacy of the room, which on ordinary occasions the girl was jealous of exposing to vulgar eyes, with its little array of photographs and family treasures. Mrs. Mills took no notice of these, but she quickly shut and fastened the window. "It's very early for you to be up. Don't you know it's very awkward for the servants, Miss Asquith, when a young lady takes to getting up at these unearthly hours?"

"I did not mean to trouble anybody. I heard a step, and I opened the window to see what it was."

"Dear me!" said the housekeeper; "I shouldn't have done that. What a daring thing for a young lady to do! Supposing it had been housebreakers, and your window so nice and handy for them to step into the house?"

"Do you think it was housebreakers?" Hetty cried.

"Bless you, my child, no, not in daylight. They're not as bold as that. But another time, Miss Asquith, take my advice, and don't open your window in that confiding way. You're always a deal safer with everything shut. And there are always sounds about an old house like this. For my part, I never pay any attention. Have everything well shut and fastened, and then you can't take any harm, whoever may be about."

"I thought perhaps," said Hetty, timidly, "there might be some danger—that it might be right to call some one—that I ought to ring the bell, or something."

"Bless me!" said the housekeeper again. "You would be as good as an extra watchman for the family. But look here, my dear young lady, don't you take any trouble. What is the house to you? You're only a stranger in it. Shut up your window and lock your door, and nothing can harm you. I'll have it done myself to-night. As for the house, there are plenty to see to that, and no danger of housebreakers here."

Hetty was very much agitated by these interviews. She found no satisfaction in them. The doctor's repeated assurance that he was always near was little more consolatory than the housekeeper's injunctions to shut herself up, and take no concern for the house. Hetty could not understand anything of the kind. To be shut up in shivering safety, a poor little atom of terrified consciousness in the midst of unknown dangers, indifferent to and shut off from everybody around, seemed to her so unnatural, so horrible. She remembered now the chill she had felt when she heard Miss Hofland lock her door. Was it possible to live in a house like this—each shut in, safe under lock and key, and no one taking any interest in the panic or trouble which might be in the next room?

This thought was more strange to Hetty than even the thought of danger. Danger! She had known what it was to feel a thrill of terror when she woke in the night and heard some of those sounds which are always alarming to a watcher: the vague noises of the darkness, sounds exaggerated by the surrounding silence into something inexplicable, mysterious creaks and cracklings. But then there was the sense of habitation in the house, the certainty of father and mother always ready to be appealed to, and at whose appearance all dangers were disarmed. At Horton the sensation was very different. The house felt empty, cold, with a mysterious chill in it, and a few trembling individuals dotted along the side of the house, each shut up in her separate room. This was more dreadful to Hetty than words could say. She was very silent all day, shivering from time to time, extremely pale, as unlike the bright-faced girl she had been a little while before as it is possible to conceive. And they were all very kind. Miss Hofland flew to her favourite idea of a headache and to her favourite expedient of lying on the sofa, which was her panacea for all troubles. "I'll get you a book, my dear," she said. "I have a very nice book, which I brought with me. I am sure you have never read it; and now you can lie quite comfortably, and not be disturbed by anything. Going to bed may be better when you have a headache; some people think so: but it is giving in so when you go to bed, and then it's lonely, and unless you can sleep, I don't see the advantage. You are just as well on the sofa, and more cheerful. I am afraid Horton is not going to agree with you: and that would be such a bore when we have just got so nicely settled down."

"I don't wonder it does not agree with her," said the housekeeper, "a young lady that sleeps with her window open in this weather."

"Oh, goodness!" cried Miss Hofland. "A window opening on the park in any weather! You must not do it, my dear. Why, anything might run in—a rabbit or a squirrel out of the woods, or one of the sheep that's grazing about, or even a cow. Fancy being woke in the middle of the night by a cow! I can't conceive what I should do—shriek till I brought the house down. Fancy a cow's breath suddenly puffed out upon you, and a great 'Mo—oo' in the middle of the night!"

"A cow's an innocent thing," said Mrs. Mills. The housekeeper kept appearing all day, coming in with every meal, keeping an eye upon Hetty. The girl felt this confusedly, though she could not think why it was.

"Oh yes! it is an innocent thing and a nice thing in its proper place. But in your bedroom at the dead of night! My dear, you must consider, if not for your own sake, yet for the sake of other people. I make it a rule to shut up my windows, even in summer. When you get used to living in strange houses that are nothing to you, where you are only for a time, you have to be particular. Why, anybody might come in—a tramp that had got into the park."

"Don't frighten the young ladies, Miss Hofland, please. There's no such thing possible. A tramp could no more get in here than at Windsor Castle. It would be as much as their places were worth to the lodge-keepers. And it's a thing that never happened. No, it's an old house, and if any one says there are noises about, that can't be quite accounted for, well, I'll not go against them: but as for tramps!" Mrs. Mills cried, with a laugh. The derision in her tone seemed to Hetty to be addressed to herself. What a little fool you are! but at least keep it to yourself, that look seemed to say.

And at night, when they all went to bed, both Miss Hofland and the housekeeper went with Hetty to her room. The latter had given instructions to the housemaid, and everything was fastened in Hetty's room, the shutters closed, the curtains drawn, a dreadful sense of being shut up and cut off from everything breathing in the motionless air. Hetty gasped, with a feeling that she could not get breath. But the room was large and lofty, and not without air, so that the sensation was imaginative rather than real. There was a bright fire blazing, which made everything look cheerful. "This is what I call comfortable," Miss Hofland said. "Don't you think so too, my dear? Those nice soft curtains keep out every bit of draught. I must say they understand comfort in this house. Mine are so thick, if a gale is blowing, I never feel it in the least—and these are nearly as good. Surely you like that better than an open window at this time of the year?"

"Some people have a fad about open windows, and say you should have them all the year through. Some people have a fad about curtains. I don't blame Miss Asquith, for she's very young: but I think when a young lady is living with other people she should go by the ways of the house."

"I don't see that at all," said Miss Hofland. "If you've any sort of rights, you've a right to arrange your own room as you choose, and I have never done otherwise. A lady that has to live in other people's houses has many things to put up with, but I never should give in to that. All the same, my dear, when you sleep on the ground-floor you can't be too particular. Now lock the door after me, and you will be as snug and as safe as if you were in a box. Good-night, dear, and sleep well, and don't mind if you should hear the house tumbling down. It's no concern of ours."

With this Miss Hofland crossed the little passage to her own door, and waving her hand, shut and locked it, as Hetty could very well hear. The housekeeper retired by the other, repeating Miss Hofland's advice. "Just turn the key when I'm gone, and then you'll be sure nothing can happen to frighten you. And there's really nothing to frighten any one, only noises such as you hear in every old house."

Hetty, with a beating heart, did as she was told; and then the oppression of this shut-in solitude and silence came round her like a shroud. The curtains seemed to close round with an ominous envelopment. The straight lines of the walls, with no windows to break them, frightened her as if they were the sides of a box, as Miss Hofland had said. The girl's nerves were so strained that she burst into one of those youthful tempests of tears which relieve the bosom. She had nothing to cry for, nothing. Comfort, luxurious and elaborate, surrounded her, and no harm was near that she knew of. The fire burned cheerfully; everything was shut out that could frighten or trouble her. For what did Hetty cry, or what had she to fear?

CHAPTER XVIII

"LET ME GO HOME"

WHEN Hetty woke in the middle of the night, and found herself in darkness, without a glimmer of light, curtains and shutters closing her in, doors locked between her and all the rest of the world, a gloom which could be felt weighing down her eyelids, the sensation of terror which overwhelmed her was no doubt entirely unreasonable. Miss Hofland next door felt these precautions essential to her rest. But little Hetty lay not daring to breathe, bound in a speechless and horrible panic which no words could express. Nothing that she could have seen or heard would have equalled the horror of seeing nothing, of lying there a hopeless prisoner of the darkness, the silence throbbing round her, the gloom pressing upon her like a tangible weight. How she had woke, whether by the reverberation of some cry, or by some stirring in the night, she could not tell. She thought it was both. She thought that some shriek penetrating the too great and tingling profundity of silence, and some movement in the intense, insupportable gloom, had broken the uneasy sleep into which she had fallen against her will while the firelight lasted, with its friendly blaze and little crackling. These had saved her from the horror of the shut-up place. But now the fire had died out, there was no glimpse or glimmer anywhere; all was dark, dark, horrible, a blackness growing upon her, getting into her very soul. Something of the effect of a nightmare was in that horrible gloom. It seemed to hold her so that she could not move, and scarcely could breathe. There seemed no air, but only darkness, darkness within and around. Her eyes were useless to her, as if she had none; and her ears, which seemed strained and worn with the effort, were the only sentinels she had to warn her of any approaching evil, and tingled and throbbed, either they or that black vacancy which they watched. All this was nothing, as the reader knows, it was only a child's fantastic rendering of the most common-place fact, but to Hetty it was a fever, a nightmare, everything that was most appalling. She started up at last, defying the still greater horror of meeting or running against some awful presence hidden in the gloom, and groped about the dreadful place till she found the curtains, restraining all the time with the most frantic effort a scream which was in her throat, which only the strongest resolution kept from bursting forth. When at last she had succeeded in opening everything, and discerned with transport a pale gleam of sky, with black tree-tops tossing about it, Hetty dropped upon the floor beside the window, almost fainting with exhaustion and relief. At last here was a little light, though it was only the glimmer of midnight. It was the sky; there was one faint star in it, shining by the edge of a cloud. She was not shut up in a box of blackness and darkness and separated from all the world.

Feverish thoughts flew through Hetty's brain in this half-swoon. She said to herself, Would death be like that?—all black, nothing to be heard or seen, a horrible blank, in which nothing but throbbing terror and dread consciousness were. She tried to tell herself that death was nothing at all, only a passage from earth to heaven, but had not enough command of her faculties to follow that or any other argument, but only to feel, with a wild relief, that she was not dead, for here was the sky still palely glimmering, light in it, not blackness, as the shut-up room had been. She supposed afterwards that she had fallen asleep there, half wrapped in the curtain near that blessed window which had brought her back to life; for when she came to herself much later, in the first profound chills of dawn, she found herself half lying, half sitting, in the elastic fold of the heavy curtain, aching with cold and exposure, and for the moment deeply wondering how she came there, at the foot of the tall window which was now full of the grey lightness of the coming day.

Hetty was paler than ever, nervous, and trembling, next day. She had caught a chill, everybody said; and again Miss Hofland prescribed the sofa, the novel, hot cups of tea, and other gratifications; the lessons were done by her side to save her trouble, and little Rhoda showed her a great deal of silent sympathy, stealing to her side in the intervals of those simple studies, putting an arm round her neck as she stood by the sofa, even bestowing a silent kiss by way of consolation. The girl recovered her courage during the day, especially as the sun shone, and everything looked brighter. But as evening drew near, Hetty paled and shivered once more. "A cold is always worse in the evening," said Miss Hofland, and recommended bed earlier than usual, and a hot drink. Bed was the thing of all others that Hetty feared. She lay on the sofa by the comfortable fire in a state of confused and self-reproachful misery, such as only the very young are capable of feeling. Words seemed on her very lips which she with difficulty kept from becoming audible. "Oh, let me go home to mamma! oh, let me go home! let me go home!" She thought if she once began saying it, she would have to go on and on and never

101

could stop herself. "Oh, let me go home!" She said it over and over and over within herself, but was checked continually by the thought that if she said it aloud, if she could have her wish, there would be an end of all that had been dreamed of, of the bills that might be paid, and the sealskin for mamma. Hetty bought the sealskin dear. It was that above all that kept her dumb, that kept down that cry, "Oh, let me go to mamma!" But then mamma would go cold in her thin cloak all next winter, because Hetty could not command herself. It came to a compromise at last in a fit of nervous sobbing, which she could not restrain when, after Rhoda had been sent away, Miss Hofland again proposed going to bed.

"My dear! what is the matter? Do you feel ill? Have you a sore throat? I do hope you are not going to be hysterical. My dear child, do get the better of that crying. Tell me frankly what's the matter. If it's anything I can help you in, I will do it; but, for goodness' sake, don't sob like that. What is it you want, my dear?"

"Oh, Miss Hofland, I don't know. I suppose it's only mamma. I feel as if I couldn't do without mamma."

"Oh, you poor child! Well, I have heard a great many girls say that, my dear. It's common when you're beginning your life. I never had any mother, and I used to envy them with their crying. I'd have given a great deal to have had anything to cry for. But every one has to be reasonable in the end, and you have a great deal of sense, my dear. You wouldn't have been sent away unless they had thought it was best for you. Now isn't that true? You must just make up your mind to it, and put up with it, till the time comes; and then all will be right, and you'll get back."

"Yes, I know; I can't help saying it, Miss Hofland, but I don't really want it. I want to—stay out my time, and—and get my—money," Hetty said, keeping down her sobs.

"Yes, that is the right way to look at it," said the governess. She understood well enough, having seen it so often, the little sudden access of home-sickness, the heroic childish resolution to bear up to the end and get the money, which so often means far more than money to the young creature who earns it. Miss Hofland patted Hetty's shoulder, and soothed her with genuine feeling; and then she fell into the tone of one far older than Hetty, and which she truly called governessy. "Besides, my dear," she said, "you must recollect that if you are to be from home at all, you couldn't be in a more comfortable house. It's a little queer, and I can't help thinking that some day or other something will be found out to account for it: but they treat us very well; that can't be denied. In some places they don't allow you a fire in your room, and the schoolroom dinners are like nursery meals, only not so plentiful. It is a great addition to all the other things you have to put up with when that's the case. But here everything is very comfortable. Your mother would be quite pleased if she saw how everything is arranged for us here."

Hetty's sobs died away under the influence of this speech—whether it was the good sense in it, or that the mode of consolation adopted was so entirely unfitted to the trouble, a thing which sometimes has quite a good effect.

"And then, you know," said Miss Hofland, "there's the satisfaction of knowing that whatever there may be that is strange and out of the way, it doesn't concern us. They say that other people's misfortunes make you enjoy your own comforts the more. I wouldn't go quite so far as that: but it is a great gratification to reflect, when you are in a house where there is evidently a skeleton somewhere or other, that it is no business of yours. There's no telling the comfort there is in that.'

"But, Miss Hofland," said Hetty, "do you think that just to lock your door, and never to mind whatever may happen to the house, as Mrs. Mills says——"

"Is that what she says?" said the governess, quickly. "Oh, you may be sure that's not her way; she would be at the bottom of it. I'm confident, whatever it was, they couldn't conceal anything from her! But she's got a good deal in her, that woman, though I don't like her, my dear. I shouldn't say but it would be the wisest thing, on the whole. For what could you do? You can't clear up their mysteries or put things straight, so why should you give yourself any trouble? If you thought there were signs of fire, indeed, why then of course you should give the alarm at once; for we all should suffer from that, we poor ladies who have nothing to do with it, and the servants and all. Yes, I should always give the alarm, whatever it cost you, in case of a fire; but for other things I am not sure that she did not give you the very best advice. A man, if he heard a noise, would have to get up and see what it was; but a lady may always lock her door. I do it invariably wherever I am, my dear. In the first place, it's safer, for you never know who might come blundering into your room, as I told you this morning; and then it frees you from a great deal of responsibility. As a rule, at the outset of your career, I should say that Mrs. Mills gave you very good advice."

Hetty's attention failed while Miss Hofland ran on. She lost reckoning of the motives presented to her, the rule of conduct which her companion would have been the first to call governessy. Another subject was foremost in Hetty's thought—her own room,

103

into which she was about to be taken as into a prison, where all would be black again, as before, and the doors locked, everybody's door locked, so that if any stronger horror should seize her, there was nowhere she could fly to, no one to whom she could escape and be safe. She was glad the governess should talk, in order to put off that evil hour as long as possible. Miss Hofland sat over the fire, quietly flowing forth in that philosophy of the dependent, how to keep safest in a sort of camp by yourself in the midst of an ungenial, if not unfriendly, world, how to avoid responsibility and secure calm, however those around you might be agitated. This was the code of things expedient which had been fixed in her mind by years of experience. The girl listened very vaguely at first, and then went off altogether into her own individual alarms. Her pretty, comfortable room, with its pleasant fire, that luxury which was not always allowed, had once more become a dark prison-house to Hetty. How was she to go through such another night?

There was a glimmer of comfort in the fact that Miss Hofland accompanied her there, to see that her hot footbath was ready, and her hot drink. "You must just jump into bed and cover yourself up warm, and never budge till morning; and you'll see your cold will be ever so much better," she said, tapping Hetty upon the cheek affectionately. "Now, my clear, don't be a little goose." And then Hetty, with anguish which she could scarcely contain, heard her go into her room and turn the key. "It frees you from a great deal of responsibility," she had said. And how was she to know the miserable panic that was in the poor little girl's heart, left thus alone with her consciousness of wanderers outside and mysteries within, and the sense of darkness and imprisonment, and no one within call, whatever might happen? Hetty's first wild idea was that it would be better to sit up all night, and thus cheat the black gloom and silence that lay in wait for her. But she was very obedient and quite unused to act for herself; and there seemed to her something guilty, something dreadful, in thus disregarding all the usages of life. She sat down by her fire and read for as long a time as she could keep her attention to her novel, and then, trembling to find it was midnight, she stole to bed at last. Happily, she was so worn out that she slept immediately, as if there had been no panics or mysteries in the world, or as if her mother's room—that shelter from all harm—had been open to her next door.

CHAPTER XIX

IN THE DEAD OF NIGHT

"OH no! my dear young lady, no no; you must not be so easily discouraged. Our little friend is very fond of you, and everybody likes you. Come! you must try and put up with us a little longer. You must get back your pretty colour and throw off this nasty little fever. The will has a great deal to do with it, hasn't it, Darrell? Come, Miss Hester! You must not make your mamma think we have been unkind to you; that would never do," the kind old clergyman said.

"That is what I am always telling her," said Miss Hofland. "She is too old, you know, to cry after her mother; and I tell her I used to envy the girls that had something to cry for, for I never had any mother. I might have cried my eyes out, and it wouldn't have done me any good."

"Dear, dear!" said the old Rector, looking at the governess with a mixture of wonder and alarm, a momentary tribute to her cleverness in getting into the world by some unknown way; and then he returned to Hetty, patting her affectionately upon the shoulder. "She's not too old for anything," he said soothingly. "She's too young for anything, and never was away from her dear mother before: I feel sure she never knew what it was——"

"My dear! before the Rector and Mr. Darrell!" cried Miss Hofland. "You ought to have a little proper pride."

For Hetty, hearing all these allusions to her mother and the talk that went on over her, and being very weak and in a paroxysm of excited feeling, had given way to a tempest of tears.

"Let her cry," said the kind old Rector, still going on patting her with an almost mesmeric touch. "It must get vent, you know, and better here than when she is alone. Just leave her to me a little, and she will come round. You know, my dear young lady, if it should fall to your lot in this world to get your own living, as many a nice, good girl has to do, there are always difficulties to be got over at first. It's not like home. Though you put ever so good a face upon it, it's not like home. When you get used to it, you take the bitter with the sweet. But I have often seen at the beginning that there was a little crisis, and it was touch and go whether the poor little young heart could face the lot or not."

"Oh yes," cried Hetty convulsively; "it is not that; it's only that I'm feeling—ill; it is not that I am—silly: indeed, indeed!" the poor child cried, struggling to speak steadily.

"It is only this, that she is feverish, and her nerves have received a shock," said the young doctor. "Now that the days are brightening, and she can get out in the open air——"

The little old clergyman nodded his head and went on, "I understand all that. But all the same there's this little crisis which has to be got over. I daresay, my dear, that Miss Hofland had it too, though she tells us that she never had what most people have. I was once a tutor in my young days, and I felt it, though I was a man. There are particular qualities that are wanted for this dependent sort of life. We are all more or less dependents here," he said, looking round benevolently upon the group about him. The speech was very well meant, but it was not very well received: the young doctor made a hasty step apart, as if to separate himself from the others, while Miss Hofland cried, "Oh, Mr. Rector!" with suppressed indignation, "I do not consider myself a dependent. I have accepted a position for a year, and so long as I do the duties I've undertaken, I hope I'm as independent as any one. I don't mix myself up with the family at all," Miss Hofland said.

"Well, my dear young lady," said the old clergyman, "I am, if nobody else is: for though I am called the Rector by most people, and though I have been here for a great number of years, I am only here, after all, as locum tenens, which is a name you will no doubt have heard, as a clergyman's daughter; that means, you know, that I am here enjoying all my little comforts at the will and pleasure of somebody else. He might send me away to-morrow, or at least in three months' time: or he might die. He has been expected to die a great many times. I think sometimes he never will. He's an old, old fellow, much older that I am, and I, though I am an old man, am quite dependent upon him, so, you see, I know what I am talking about."

"Oh, Mr. Rector, if that is what you mean!" murmured Miss Hofland, abashed.

"Papa was the same once," said Hetty, roused out of her self-occupation. "We had a delightful house and a great, beautiful garden. But then the old gentleman died, and we had to give it up."

"When my old gentleman dies, I shall have to give it up too; but I hope he will outlive me. When an old man like that gets up among the eighties, he may just as well live for ever: and I'm sure I hope he will. So, you see, I have a long experience of being dependent; and I should like to give you the help of my experience, you who are at the other end. But I hope you will not have to live this kind of life."

"You needn't feel any dependence unless you please," said Miss Hofland. "I would not set her against it, Mr. Rector, if she should have to follow it, for a girl in most cases cannot choose for herself."

"I don't mean to set her against it," said the old clergyman; but they were both interrupted by Hetty, to whom this opening of a new interest was invaluable.

"If this old gentleman is so old," she said, "I wonder what his name is? I wonder if perhaps he is the old Rector, Uncle Hugh, that mamma used to tell us about?"

The little group round Hetty was thunder-struck by this remark. Miss Hofland hastily took up the eau-de-cologne, with a glance of alarm; and the doctor lifted his head sharply and fixed his eyes upon her, as if with a sudden gleam of hope.

"Uncle Hugh!" cried the old clergyman. "My dear Miss Hester—I—this is very surprising. He is Mr. Hugh Prescott, certainly, if you happen to mean that."

"Oh," cried Hetty, with awakened interest, "then it is Uncle Hugh! Mamma has not heard of any of them for such a long time. She says it is so wrong not to keep up writing, but there are so many of us, and she has so much to do. Then Uncle Hugh is still alive! I will write directly and tell her. She will be so pleased to know."

"Then your mother is——? To be sure!" cried the old clergyman. "Asquith! I ought to have remembered. It is not so common a name but that I might have remembered. Your father was once the curate here." He looked round upon his companions with a strange look, as if admitting some new possibility from which unknown combinations might arise. "Why, she's a relation of the family," he said.

The housekeeper had come into the room while this conversation was going on. She was always coming and going; and it was a great grievance with Miss Hofland that she had begun constantly to open the door without knocking, which was an assertion of equality on the housekeeper's part which the governess could not bear. She came forward now with a cup of chicken-broth for Hetty, and in a moment became somehow the central figure in the group. "Of the old family," she said firmly, "and that is what I have always thought. I thought from the beginning that there was more than met the eye in that young lady being here."

The doctor stepped forward quickly, giving the woman a hasty, warning look. "I wish I had known before," he said. "It might have made things easier." And then he stopped, both in

107

words and action, as if suddenly perceiving either that he had said too much, or that his confusion had betrayed him into something which ought not to have been said at all. "To be sure, I don't see that it makes much difference," he said between his teeth.

"I think," said the housekeeper, somewhat severely, "that if you will reflect a moment, you will see that it makes no difference at all."

Miss Hofland, who was entirely in the dark, looked from one to another with bewilderment. "Do you mean that Hetty is a relation of little Rhoda?" she cried.

"The Rector said, Miss Hofland, of the old family," said the housekeeper pointedly; but neither of the gentlemen spoke. A curious silence fell over the little party, as if no one, except Mrs. Mills, whose views were peremptory, understood what was to be made of this new idea, whether it were of great importance or of no importance at all. It did not end in any additional demonstrations towards Hetty, to whom indeed, in the little lingering illness, which, after all, was no more than a feverish cold, aggravated by the tortures of the imagination which she had been going through, and which Dr. Darrell only partly guessed at, everybody had been as kind as it was possible to be. The housekeeper herself, though so severe and secretly distrusted by all the party, had been very kind to Hetty. If it had been the daughter of the house, as Miss Hofland remarked, there could not have been more pains taken with her. "Certainly they do treat us very well; there is nothing whatever to be found fault with in that respect." But no doubt Miss Hofland herself looked upon the girl with a different eye. A relation of the old family! The governess at least entertained from the beginning the conviction, formed at once on her entry on her duties, that the old family was very much superior to the new.

As for Hetty herself, this little discovery did her more good than the chicken-broth. It raised her failing spirit; it gave the pleasant impulse of a new event. It was indeed, when she came to think of it, no event at all, for though it had not seemed necessary to speak of it to the servants and dependents of the new family, or to the little heiress who was all she was acquainted with of the new family, Hetty herself had been aware from the first that the house in which she was living was the house of her ancestors, and that probably, as she thought, she had far more to do with it, and certainly with the old pictures, than Rhoda had, to whom everything would some day belong. There were no old servants in the establishment who could remember her mother, no sign of any one recollecting that such an unusual name as that of Asquith had once been known at Horton. But now that the discovery had come about in this natural way, it pleased Hetty. She had not written much to her mother since she had been ill; but now, in the pleasant excitement of her discovery, it was the first thing she thought of. As soon as the visitors went away, she got up from her sofa of her own accord, forgetting her dizziness and weakness, and began to write a little. "Such a discovery has been made," she wrote. "Uncle Hugh is alive still, he is living abroad for his health, and the Rector is only locum tenens, as papa was at Retford. He hopes Uncle Hugh may live for ever, but that is not very likely, is it? My cold is a great deal better. I think hearing this has driven it away; not that it makes much difference, but still it makes one feel one's self more at home, and as if the house really did belong to us once." After she had written this cheerful letter, Hetty spent the most cheerful evening she had known for a long time. Her fever seemed to have flown; her hands were moist; a little soft pink colour came back to the cheeks which had alternated between red and white. The sense of being better is in itself the best of medicines. It went on raising her courage, strengthening her nerves, making her altogether like herself. She went to sleep tranquilly, without any alarm or excitement, with the shutters folded back a little, the curtains drawn back, and one line of the light she loved, one little span of sky, looking in upon her, so that she could see it where she lay. It was a moonlight night, very soft, the temperature having risen, and everything, as Miss Hofland said, "turning for the best."

It might be the middle of the night, veering towards the morning, when that calm was disturbed. The moon had gone down, and it was still long before dawn: the darkness intense, the softness of the evening lost in the dead chill and depth of night, and, so far as any one was aware, the great house of Horton all silent, filled with sleep and quiet—when suddenly a wild and terrible shriek pealed through the stillness, a cry that might have waked the dead, a cry of terror past reason, almost past humanity, shrill and awful; it was followed by two others in swift succession, cutting the silence like stabs of a weapon. It takes much to wake a house so wrapped in quiet, in the midst of its night's sleep; but there was an instantaneous awakening in one quarter of the house, which helped to rouse the rest; and when Miss Hofland, too much startled by the keen ring of that shriek, almost at her very door, to think of her own philosophy of precaution, hurried out into the passage in consternation, her hair hanging over her shoulders, her naked feet thrust into slippers, she met with a second shock almost as great as the first, the housekeeper in her usual trim

109

dress hurrying towards Hetty's door with a candle in her hand. This sight transfixed the dishevelled maids, who, taking courage from their numbers, were rushing from all sides crying, "What is it? Who is it?" with shrieks almost as noisy, though so wonderfully different in intensity, from that which had awakened the house. The governess was aware of the second bewilderment, though she did not pause to think what it was. A blast of cold air came in their faces, as they burst into Hetty's room, from the window, one side of which stood open, like a door, into the profoundest midnight darkness. On the bed lay Hetty, or her ghost—a white face with staring eyes, with the bedclothes drawn up tightly as if with an effort to pull them over her face in her two clenched and rigid hands. Her eyes stared wide open, but there was no meaning in them; the mouth still seemed to quiver with that shriek, but was capable of no utterance. The horror of some sight unspeakable seemed to linger in the awful lines about the staring eyes, and in the wild hollows of the marble cheeks—marble white, and with the rigidity of marble too. A murmur of horror came from the women, cowed at the sight, except Mrs. Mills, who held up her candle, throwing a strange light upon the paralysed face. The candle trembled in her hand, but she uttered no word. It was thought afterwards that this was what she had expected to see.

And presently, running in hot haste, with every mark of agitation, pale, with the perspiration pouring down his face, as if he had been engaged in some mortal struggle, the young doctor in his ordinary dress came down the corridor and entered Hetty's room. He had the tail of his coat half torn off at one side, the governess remarked, as, remembering her own undressed condition, she took refuge behind the curtain. The young man flung himself down on his knees by the bedside, calling out to the housekeeper to hold her candle low, and loosening or trying to loosen the rigid hands. "Is she dead, Doctor? Is she dead?" Mrs. Mills said in a low voice of horror. She trembled in every limb, but she was not surprised.

CHAPTER XX

A MIDNIGHT VISITOR

THIS was what had happened to Hetty.

In the middle of the night she had woke up suddenly as on that occasion when she had come to life out of her dreams, and felt the intolerable darkness go chill to her very soul. What it was that awakened her, whether sound or sensation, the rush of the cold night air, or only some consciousness of trouble and horror, she never could tell. She woke, but not to darkness this time. Her eyes went to the light instinctively—to the faint long opening of the window, which though all moonlight was gone still marked itself upon the darkness around. She woke with a gasp and suppressed cry. Her first sensation was the freshness of the air, which showed that her window was open, and then that something moved in that lighter space through which the wind blew. A terror, to which all her previous fright seemed only preliminary, a horror of anticipation and certainty, froze her very soul. Whatever it was, it had come, it had her at last. She lay paralyzed, not able to move; her eyes, the only capable things in her, straining into that dimness, a little lighter than the darkness, where something unformed and horrible moved: moved! that could be no delusion. She saw it with all the clearness of her young, keen faculties, strung into the most dreadful acuteness of perception—not what it was, but that it moved, now blocking the faint grey, wavering in it, moving out of it, in, into the darkness of her room, near her, close to her. Hetty lay motionless, in a trance of unspeakable terror. What it was she could not say. It would have been less horrible had she been able to see it. It was something that moved, that was all. And then there followed faint, stealthy sounds as if of contact with the furniture, like some one groping in the dark: and suddenly that dreadful something moved close to her, between her and the window, touching the line of her bed. It wavered, seemed to pass, then turned back. The miserable child did not breathe, kept still with one last effort, turned to stone by delirious fear. But something, the subtle consciousness that breathes from every living creature, betrayed her in the portentous gloom. Suddenly she felt something; a hand—was it a hand?—passed over her face; and then the thing, which was not distinct enough to be called a shadow, dropped by her bedside, and drew close—close with the breath of another human creature, upon her. "My child, my little

111

darling, my little darling! I've found you, I've found you at last!" The breath, the voice, the touch of the cold hand, turned Hetty's brain. And then it was that those shrieks arose, the indescribable, toneless, sharp discords, the cry of mortal terror passed into delirium; and she knew no more.

"She is not dead," said Mr. Darrell, examining with the candle the horrible, fixed, staring eyes that saw nothing, that were unconscious of his examination and undazzled by the light. "She is not dead. I am not sure that she isn't worse than dead."

"How did it happen?" said the housekeeper, in quick, low tones.

"How can I tell you?—negligence! Get hot water, hot irons—anything that is handiest. We must bring back the circulation, if that is possible. Oh, thank you!" The young doctor threw a vague glance at the white figure that suddenly appeared from behind the curtains, and got into the bed beside Hetty's marble form. He did not recognise who it was. "That's the best thing you can do; rub her feet, get the blood back anyhow—anyhow. Get hot water, some of you, quick! Go on with that while I go and get something for her."

The housekeeper laid her hand upon him as he was hurrying away. "Is all safe?" she asked in her low, quick voice. "Are you sure all's safe?"

"Yes, yes," he said impatiently; "what's that in comparison with this?"

"It's our first business all the same," said the woman. The young doctor made a despairing movement of his hand towards the bed and hurried away.

Miss Hofland had taken the girl's inanimate figure into her arms. "I'm almost too cold myself to be of any use to her," she said, shivering at the contact of the frozen limbs. Mrs. Mills put down her candle by the bedside, where it threw a strange side light upon that tragic mask on the pillow, with the open mouth and staring, awful eyes. Was it Hetty? Was it possible it could be Hetty? All human identity as of feature, or age, or character seemed to have gone out of the rigid face. The housekeeper had her wits all about her—the self-command, Miss Hofland instinctively reflected, of a person not taken by surprise. She gave a few orders to the frightened women, who stood huddled together staring at the foot of the bed, to shut the window, to light fires and prepare hot water. Then she came back to the bedside, quite cool, professional, unexcited. "If it's cataleptic, all we can do won't make much difference," she said calmly: and proceeded to open the clenched hands, and disengage the coverings which were held as in a vice.

"Ah!" said Mrs. Mills, "she's not so unconscious as she looks. She resisted me then—only a little—but still she resisted. She's coming round."

"How can it have happened?" Miss Hofland asked. She had got over her first fright and horror, and to talk over a patient, however alarming may be his or her state, is a temptation which nurses, when there are two of them, can rarely resist. They were full of human kindness and interest, and doing everything for her that could be done; but their very interest and anxiety found relief in this discussion of the case.

"Who can tell? She had left her window open again. She never could be cured of that. Her mother must have some fad about open windows."

"Then you think some one must have come in?"

"Some one? Who was there to come in? Something—perhaps one of the cattle or something—meaning no harm; or perhaps she only imagined it. Imagination is rather worse than fact."

"I said a cow," said Miss Hofland thoughtfully. "It would be very strange finding a cow by your bedside in the middle of the night: it might be any sort of a monster: but, goodness! not to overwhelm a girl like that! I think she's not quite so cold. I think she's not quite so rigid. Hetty, wake up, my dear!"

"Let her alone," said the housekeeper. "She can't hear you. If we get her circulation back, that will be the best chance."

"But how could it have happened?" repeated Miss Hofland, "for I don't much believe in the cow. I can't say I believe in the cow. Oh, how her poor eyes stare! Do you believe she doesn't see, though she stares so? Hetty! oh, shake it off, darling, shake it off! If you will only make an effort!"

"What is the use?" said Mrs. Mills. "She can't hear you. If she could, it would be bad for her to be roused so. Young Darrell is very clever, they say; he'll do all that can be done."

"He looked as if he knew what it was."

"Oh, hush, here he is coming back! don't let him hear you," cried the housekeeper, and then the colloquy came to an end.

But the case was not so simple as Miss Hofland thought. No power of making an effort remained in poor little Hetty. Her previous terrors, which had been chiefly of the imagination, had undermined her strength. She had no longer any force to resist this overwhelming horror when it came. Whether it was her intelligence which had been killed by the blow, whether she were only stunned temporarily, or if it was a moral paralysis of the whole being which had laid her low, could not be divined. She came round a little from that first trance. After a time her eyes

113

could close, her breathing began to be faintly audible, the rigidity of her limbs relaxed. After a longer interval she came to herself so much as to say "Thank you" faintly to the nurses, and to swallow, though with difficulty, the nourishment they administered. During this period there had been the greatest difficulty in satisfying Hetty's correspondents at home. She had already fallen out of her early punctuality in respect to letter-writing, which smoothed matters a little; but when day by day went by without producing any amelioration in her state, and when letters began to rain upon the house at Horton full of demands for explanation, and to know what was the matter, Mr. Darrell one day announced to the housekeeper with some haste, and an unnecessary sharpness of tone, "I'll tell you what it is. I'm going to send for her mother, and that without delay."

Mrs. Mills looked up in consternation. "Her mother!" she cried. "The last woman in the world to come here!"

"She may be the last woman or anything else you please, but she is the only person that has anything to do here, and I am going to send for her. Look there! do you think that can be allowed to go on?" the young man cried, turning half round to where Hetty sat like a waxen image, supported by cushions in a chair. She lay back as white as the pillow upon which her head rested, her eyelids flickering now and then, her thin hands crossed in her lap. She made no complaint, said scarcely anything except that feeble "Thank you," when anything was brought her, or when some of her anxious attendants paused to smooth her cushions, or ask if she wanted anything. It was a sight to melt the hardest heart.

"And it is more than a week since it happened," said young Darrell, "and that is all we have been able to do. You are an excellent nurse, Mrs. Mills; you have neglected nothing: and Miss Hofland does everything that kindness can suggest: but you see yourself that we make no progress. I can do nothing more; her mother may."

"Time will make it all right," the housekeeper said. "Of course I am very sorry—I would give anything that it had not happened. Of course the poor little thing has got a dreadful shock. But she is very young, and in time she will get all right."

"If you like to trust to time with such a delicate thing as a girl's life," said the young doctor, "I don't. We must do something. Either that and try the effect of nature, or else I must have the best authority from town to see her; and you know what questions a physician would ask, and perhaps you know how we could answer him. I don't."

"Mr. Darrell," said the housekeeper, "you're my superior. I

have to take my orders from you. All the same, I consider that our first business is to look after what we were put here for. I cannot acknowledge that a child frightened, even though she is frightened into fits, is any reason for giving up."

"There are a hundred reasons for giving up," cried the young man passionately. "I would give up this moment if I could, if there was any one to give up my charge to. It's neither right nor necessary, what we're doing. I have never stopped regretting I undertook it, never since——"

"Say the truth, Mr. Darrell, never since—this young lady came here! I've seen it from the first. She's not much more than a child, but you think more of her than of every one else in the house."

The young doctor blushed like a girl to the very roots of his hair. "I have no intention of answering any such accusation," he said. "It is entirely uncalled for, and quite unjustifiable. I have done my duty to the utmost, if such a charge could ever be any one's duty. My doubts have a very different foundation. But I don't go so far as to sacrifice life to my engagements, and therefore I'm going to telegraph to Mrs. Asquith to beg her to come here at once, without an hour's delay."

"Then I'll telegraph to Mrs. Rotherham," said the housekeeper. "Oh, dear! she is so far away. How can you betray a poor lady that is so far away? I'll send for the lawyer. It was he that brought this girl here, and he had better come and take her away. Yes, that's it. Let's make a compromise, Doctor. Send her away. To go home, of course, is the best thing for her. Change of air, and change of scene, and her own folks—that's far, far better. I'll run the chance of whatever she may say when she gets better. Let us send her away."

Mr. Darrell turned and looked again at the motionless figure in the chair. His face softened into the deepest, tender pity. "If you think what she was when she came here," he said, "all full of life and spirit, and to look at her now, like a withered flower! No. I can't take the responsibility of sending her away. Her mother, or a physician, one or the other! I can't have her life and her reason to answer for all alone. I am going to telegraph to Mrs. Asquith, now."

The housekeeper stopped him, catching at his arm. "Do you know who Mrs. Asquith is?" she said.

"Mr. Tenby told me—a relation. Well, so much the better. I am sick of my share in it," cried the young man. They had been standing talking at the window. Hetty had been moved to another room on the other side of the house, where nothing could remind

115

her of the terrible incident which had changed her whole being, and which was lighted by a large recessed window. He left the housekeeper standing there, and went up to the girl, sitting motionless in her chair. "Is there anything you would like?" he said. "Can I get you anything? Shall I move you nearer the window? Do you think you would like to see any one? Shall I call Miss Hofland? Is there any one whom you would like me to call?" There was a faint hope in his mind that she would say "Mamma," which she had cried so piteously at first. But Hetty said nothing save "Thank you," with the faintest movement of her lips.

CHAPTER XXI

AN INNOCENT SUFFERER

THE house had never been a lively house, but it had turned into the dreariest of habitations now. All those comforts which Miss Hofland had felt to make up for so much did not compensate for the absence of Hetty, or what was worse, for the presence of Hetty, spell-bound in that great chair, and for the innocent questions of Rhoda, who asked and asked, every new demand being but an echo of the questions which already were thrilling through the governess's heart. "But why?" Rhoda said. "What made her like that? What has happened to her? Things can't happen, can they, without a cause? Why has Hetty turned like that? She was never like that before. If you will not tell me I will ask Mr. Darrell; he is the doctor, and he must know."

"She got some dreadful fright, my dear. Don't speak to Mr. Darrell, for I don't think he knows; and if he does know, he would not tell a little girl like you."

But this answer did not satisfy Rhoda. She caught Mr. Darrell, as it happened, exactly at this moment when he was going out. "Oh, Mr. Darrell, I want you to tell me what has made Hetty like that. What is the matter with Hetty? Oh, yes, I have seen her. Do you think they could shut her up and hide her from me? Mr. Darrell, what has happened to Hetty? You are the doctor, and you must know."

"The doctor doesn't know everything," he said.

"But very near everything," said Rhoda. "She is very ill, I am sure. Tell me what it is, and I won't trouble you any more."

"I can't tell what it is," said the young doctor. "I wish I could, then perhaps I might know how to make her better. I am going now to send for some one who perhaps can do it. It is only perhaps, but I am going to try."

"Another doctor?" asked Miss Hofland. "I can understand that you don't like the responsibility. I shouldn't if I were in your place."

"Not another doctor, at present, but her mother," Mr. Darrell said; and he went off and left them, though it was scarcely civil to do so, when they had so many questions to ask.

"Her mother!" Rhoda said, pondering. "Is it a good thing to bring her mother? What good can her mother do her? She is not a

117

doctor. I should think Mr. Darrell himself would be more good than that."

"Oh, my dear, the very sight of your mother makes such a difference when there is anything the matter with you," said Miss Hofland. "At least," she added presently, "all the girls say so. I never had one, for my part."

Rhoda looked up at her with intelligent but unfathomable eyes, and said nothing. It appeared that the words did not bring any warmer response from Rhoda's heart.

But it would be vain to attempt to describe the agitation and trouble which was caused in the parsonage by Mr. Darrell's telegram. "Will Mrs. Asquith come at once? Daughter ill, not dangerous, but critical. Carriage will meet nine-thirty train."

"It must be something very bad," Mary said.

"No, my dear, I hope not. 'Not dangerous, but critical.' You must not frighten yourself. You must husband your strength," said the parson; but he spoke with a forced voice, and had grown very pale, paler indeed than she was; for she had so many things to think of, and he thought only of Hetty—poor little Hetty, papa's pet, as they always called her—ill and far from home.

"You must take charge of the little ones, Janey. You must not let them make a noise or annoy papa; you must see that the boys have their breakfast in good time for school, and don't let Mary Jane oversleep herself. Papa will let you have the little clock with the alarum in your room."

"Oh yes, mamma! I will try and remember everything," said Janey among her tears.

"Get in the books every week, and look over them carefully. Don't let anything be put down that we haven't had—you know how careless people are sometimes; and above all keep the house quiet when papa is in his study. You know the importance of that."

"Oh, mamma!" said Janey, "do you think then that you shall be so very, very long away?"

"I hope I maybe back again to-morrow, or the day after to-morrow," said Mary briskly. "It will depend upon how I find her. I don't doubt in the least home will be the best thing for her; but in case I should be detained," she said smiling, with her eyes very bright and liquid, each about to shed a tear, "it is so much better to mention everything. Of course I shall write; but, Janey dear, you know you have not the habit of minding everything as—as she had——"

"Oh, mamma, why don't you say Hetty? Why don't you call her by her name? It is so awful to hear you say she, as if—as if——"

118

"Didn't I call her by her name?—my dear little Hetty, my own little girl! Oh! and to think that it was I that sent her away!"

"It isn't dangerous, Mary, we have got the doctor's word for that," said her husband.

"Oh yes, to be sure we have. I am not at all frightened. You know when anything is the matter with her she gets very down, and strangers would not understand. I am all ready, Harry. No, I don't want a cab. One of the boys can carry my bag to the station, and I would rather walk. I shall have no fatigue, you know, in the railway; it will be quite a rest for me, sitting still for so many hours."

"A third-class journey is not much of a rest," said the parson, shaking his head.

"And the carriage to meet me when I get there," said Mary with a smile; "I shall feel quite a lady again, like old times, stepping out of the third class."

Half the family went with her to the station to see her off. Janey had to deny herself and stay at home with the little ones, and keep everything in order; for Mary Jane was young, and not to be trusted all by herself. Janey felt as if her heart was wrenched out of her when mamma went away to nurse Hetty, who was ill and perhaps dying, while she must stay here and watch the little ones playing, who knew nothing about it and could not understand. To have gone with her to the train and seen her go away, as the others did, would have been something, but even that solace was denied. To the younger ones it was something like an unexpected gaiety to see mamma off, and watch the bustle of the train. They had little or no doubt that Hetty would be all right as soon as mamma went to take care of her, and the boys could not help feeling a little important as they relieved each other in carrying the bag.

Mary, for her part, when she had got into the train and smiled for the last time at the eager group, and waved her last good-bye, had a very sad half-hour in the corner, with her veil down, crying and praying for her child. But after that she tried not to think, which is one of the hardest of the habitual processes through which a mind has to go which requires to be always fit for the service of a number of others, and consequently has to keep itself well in hand. She had been obliged to do this many times before, and though it was harder than usual, now that she was alone and had no immediate occupation to take off her thoughts, yet she did more or less succeed in the effort. There was a poor weakly young mother in the carriage, going to join her sailor husband somewhere, with a troublesome baby whom she could

119

not manage. And this was a great help to Mrs. Asquith in keeping off thought and subduing the pain of anxiety. She said to herself this was one advantage of the third class. Had she been travelling luxuriously with a first-class compartment all to herself, she would not have been able to stop herself from thinking. This softened even the thrill of old associations which went through her, when, looking up as the train stopped, she perceived the little station; and, beyond it, the familiar landscape which she had not seen for so long. Was it only sixteen years? It looked like centuries, and yet not much more than a day. Nothing, however, had ever been at Horton in her time like the spruce brougham which was waiting for her, with the smart footman—smarter than any one in the service of the Prescotts had ever been. Amid all the familiarity and the strangeness Mary's heart sank within her when the servant came up. "The young lady's just the same, madam," the man said.

"Can you tell me what's the matter? Oh! can you tell me?"

"I don't know, as no one knows," said the servant, as he arranged a rug over her knees.

"Oh, if you will be so kind—as fast as you can go," said Mary.

He seemed to look at her pitifully, she thought. All better hopes, if she had any, flew at the sight. She felt now that Hetty must be dying, that the case must be desperate. This delivered her from all feeling in respect to the old house where she had been brought up, the fields, the trees, the park—everything which she had known. What did she care about these associations now? She was as indifferent as if she had been but a week away, or as if she had never seen the place before.

The doctor met her at the door, looking so grave. She prepared herself for the worst again, and entered the old home without seeing or caring what manner of place it was. "Let me explain to you before you see her, Mrs. Asquith," Darrell said, leading the way into the old library, which she knew so much better than he did.

"Oh, don't keep me from her! Let me go to my child! Don't break it to me! I can see—I can see in your face!"

"She is not in any danger," he said.

Mrs. Asquith turned upon him with a gasp, having lost all power of speech: and then the self-control of misery gave way. She dropped into the nearest chair, and saved her brain and relieved her heart by tears. "May I trust you?" she asked piteously, with her quivering lips; "Hetty, my child—is in no danger?" as soon as she was able to speak.

"None that I can discover; but she is in a very alarming state.

120

She has had a fright. It seems to have paralysed her whole being. I hope everything from your sudden appearance."

"Paralysed!"

"I don't mean in the ordinary sense of the word—turned her to stone, I should say. Oh, Mrs. Asquith, I fear you will think we have ill discharged the trust you gave us. Your daughter has been frightened out of her senses, out of herself."

Mary had risen from her seat to go to her Hetty; she stared at him for a moment, and dropped feebly back again. "Do you mean that my child—my child is—mad?" she said with horror, clasping her hands.

"Oh, no, no!" cried the young doctor. "Her mind, I hope, may not be touched. She is in a state I can't explain. She takes no notice of anything. I thought it was catalepsy at first. You will be more frightened when you see her than perhaps there is any need for being——"

"Doctor—if you are the doctor—take me to her, take me to her! that is better than explanation."

"Bear with me a little, Mrs. Asquith. I want you to come in suddenly. I want to try the shock of your appearance."

"Take me to my child!" said Mary; "I cannot bear all these preliminaries. I have a right to be with Hetty, wherever she is. Where is she? Tell me what room she is in. I know my way."

"Just one moment—one moment!" he said. He led the way to the room which had been the morning-room in Mary's day, the brightest room in the house, looking out upon the flowers, and then left her at the door. "Come in," he said, "in five minutes; throw open the door; make what noise you can—oh! forgive me— and let her see you fully. Don't come too quick. It is for her sake. If she knows you, all will go well."

"If she knows me!" cried poor Mary. These terrible words subdued her in her impatience and almost anger. She stood at the door counting the time by the beatings of her heart. Then she pushed it open, as he told her. Hetty's chair had been turned round to face the door, and she sat in it, her pale hands folded in her lap, her face, like marble, against the white pillow, her eyes looking steadily before her, with an extraordinary abstract gaze. Mary stood for a moment, herself paralysed by that strange sight, clasping her hands, with a cry of trouble and consternation. Then she flew forward and flung herself on her knees before this marble image of her child. "Hetty! Hetty! Speak to me," she cried, clasping her arms round the inanimate figure. "Hetty!" Then, with a terrible cry, "Don't you know your mother? don't you know your mother, my darling, my poor child?"

121

Mary perceived none of the people behind, watching so anxiously the effect of her entrance, which had been indeed far more effective, being entirely natural, than anything they had planned. She saw only the waxen whiteness, the unresponsive silence, of the poor little soul in prison. She went on kissing the white face, the little limp hands, pouring out appeals and cries. "Oh, my child! Oh, Hetty, Hetty! Don't you know me? I'm your mother, my darling. I've come to fetch you, to take you home. Hetty, my sweet, papa's breaking his heart for you; and poor Janey daren't even cry, dear, for she must take care of them all while you and I are away. And, Hetty, the baby, your little baby—Hetty, Hetty! my own darling! Oh, Hetty, say a word to me—say a word!"

The statue moved a little; a faint tinge of colour came into the marble face; the limp little hands unfolded, fluttered a little, made as though they would go round the mother's neck. "Mamma!" Hetty said, stammering as when a child begins to speak.

And then there awoke a chorus of voices saying, "Thank God!" The women were all over-joyed, thinking the worst was past. Darrell had said if she recognised her mother—and it was evident that she had done so. But he himself stood aloof, keeping his troubled looks out of their sight. And after Mrs. Asquith had sat by her daughter's side for hours, telling her everything as if Hetty fully understood, saying a hundred things to her—news of home, caresses, tendernesses without end—it presently became evident to all that very little real advance had been made. Hetty said, "Mamma!" as she had said, "Thank you," but she did no more.

CHAPTER XXII

MARY'S INVESTIGATIONS

MRS. ASQUITH kept to all appearance perfectly tranquil during the rest of that evening. It was a strange and affecting sight to see her by the side of Hetty's chair, talking with a smiling countenance and every appearance of ease and an unburdened heart. She kept telling all the nursery stories, all the little family jokes, every kind of trifling happy circumstance, the commonplaces of the family, to her daughter's dulled and heavy ear. The spectators could not understand this strange sight. They were anxious, but she seemed free from care. They contemplated that little marble image of poor little Hetty with piteous eyes, shaking their heads aside, and saying to each other that, after all, the appearance of her mother had not done what was hoped. But the mother sat and smiled and talked as if she had been altogether unconscious that Hetty was not as she had been. Miss Hofland, though she could not understand, though she could not approve, this strange mode of action, got interested in spite of herself in all those unknown children, and found herself softly laughing in the background at the tricks of the boys, and Janey's matronly demeanour, and the sweet little sayings of the baby. It all looked so pretty, and tender, and sweet. But how that woman could talk, and talk, and smile, and tell those stories with poor Hetty blanched and unresponsive like marble, wax—anything that you can think of which is most unlike flesh and blood, was what Miss Hofland could not understand. She felt very angry. She said to herself, "That woman has so many, she has no heart for this one;" and felt as if she loved poor Hetty better than her mother did, who showed so little feeling. Rhoda, who had stolen in when no one was looking, was, on the contrary, fascinated by Mrs. Asquith. She crept closer and closer, and at last curled herself up on the skirt of the stranger's gown like a little dog, and listened, and laughed, and clapped her hands at all those stories. "Oh, tell me a little more about little Mary! Oh! what did baby say?" Rhoda cried, pushing closer and closer. Mrs. Asquith put one arm round the child, though without looking at her. She could think even of that strange child, who had been the cause of it all, with Hetty lying motionless there!

But all this had no effect upon Hetty, the lookers-on thought. An occasional faint smile came to the corners of her mouth, something so faint, so evanescent, that it could scarcely be called a smile; a faint little colour, almost imperceptible, came upon her marble paleness; now and then she said, "Mamma!" quite inconsequently, not as an answer to anything, and the tiny hands that had been folded in her lap were folded now in one of her mother's hands, which seemed to communicate a little warmth, a little life—a poor result to have effected by the heroic measure of sending for her, and admitting a stranger, against every rule, to this secluded house. The housekeeper was very impatient of the whole business. "You did it against everything I could say; and nothing has come of it," she said.

"As for that, we can't tell yet," said the doctor, naturally taking his own part; but he was very anxious, and did not seem to have taken much comfort from the new arrival. He had gone into the library to talk it over with his coadjutor, while Hetty was being conveyed to bed. The house was very quiet, the room badly lighted, the lamp on the table bringing out the anxious expression on the young man's troubled face, and half showing the figure of the housekeeper, who stood on the other side of the table. The light fell upon her hands clasped in front, and showed her person vaguely, but her face was in the shade.

"The right thing to do would have been to send the girl off to that man who treats hysteria," she said; "he would soon have brought her to her senses. What good can the mother do?—a silly woman telling all that nonsense that the girl can't hear, and would not care for if she did! Rhoda likes it, to be sure," she said, with a short laugh; "and perhaps she thinks that to make an impression upon Rhoda, who will be an heiress, is always worth her while."

"It is no part of your business, or mine either, to judge Mrs. Asquith," young Darrell said impatiently; but there could be little doubt that he was disappointed too. The effect of the mother's first appearance had not been what he hoped.

"And here we've brought in, against all our promises, just the last person in the world that ought to be admitted into this house."

"I made no promises," said the young doctor hurriedly. "How could I on this subject? No one could have foreseen such a combination of circumstances—a near relation when we expected a stranger."

"Only a cousin," the housekeeper said quickly; "but now the thing is to get rid of her as soon as possible, and in the meantime to keep her completely in the—— Good gracious! I beg your pardon, ma'am," cried Mrs. Mills, quickly stepping out of the way.

"I knocked, but you did not hear me," said Mary. "You forget that I know my way about this house." She passed the housekeeper by, and came up to where Darrell was sitting, and drew a chair to the table near him. "I have got my poor child to bed. She looks as if she had fallen asleep; whether it is sleep or stupor I can't tell, but she is very quiet. Now will you tell me how it happened?" Mary said. Her voice was very quiet, but very serious—not the voice of one who was to be trifled with. Instinctively both the listeners perceived this. Darrell cast an anxious, almost imploring glance into the surrounding dimness of the half-lighted room, and the housekeeper stirred from one foot to the other with an involuntary motion. She had not thought much of Mrs. Asquith as an antagonist, but now she began to change her mind.

"How it happened?" said the young doctor, faltering. "I am afraid it was a fright. She got a—fright."

"We cannot tell exactly how it happened," said the housekeeper quickly, "for it happened in the middle of the night."

"But you must have some sort of understanding. A thing like that can't happen in a house without some one knowing. How was it? even if you can't tell me what it was."

"It all arose from this, ma'am," said the housekeeper, "that Miss Asquith would have her window open at night. Some people I know have fads on that subject; if I asked her once, I asked her a dozen times not to do it, but she would. She would not be guided by me."

"She left her window open all night? Well, and what happened?" Mary said.

Mr. Darrell cleared his throat. A kind of loathing of the glib woman, who was so ready to answer for him, quickened his speech. "So far as we can tell, something came into her room and frightened her," he said.

"Something? Oh! this is trifling," cried Mary impatiently. "Many, many a night have I slept in this house with my window open. The windows were always open. What is there about, to come in at an open window in the middle of the night?"

The two culprits exchanged a glance across the table. The housekeeper could see the doctor's pale face full of revelations, but he could not see hers. "That's what we don't know," she said. "Miss Hofland will tell you that she warned her just as I did. Supposing it was something quite innocent—as harmless as you please—one of the sheep in the park, or a cow! A cow's an innocent thing, but it would give you a terrible fright in the middle of the night; or even a rabbit or a squirrel," continued Mrs. Mills, getting confidence as

125

she went on; "it was one of the animals about the place, for anything we know."

"What do you know? will you tell me exactly? What roused you first? and when you went to her what did you see?"

The housekeeper shivered a little. "We found her lying on her bed, poor dear! with her eyes staring, the bedclothes clenched in her hands as if she had tried to cover her face. Oh, Mrs. Asquith! I thought the child was dead." She stopped with a half sob. "And the half of the French window wide open—it's not a sash window in that room—standing wide open, showing how it had come in."

"How what had come in?" said Mary huskily, scarcely able to command her voice.

"How can I tell? Some wild creature out of the woods—some of the animals that had got loose about the farm."

"Was there any trace of an animal? There must have been some trace!"

"Or it might," said the housekeeper with a sob, the strong excitement of the moment gaining upon her, "have been a tramp that had hidden about the place."

Mary pushed her chair from the table, and covered her face with her hands. But it was only for a moment. She came back to herself, and to the examination of these unwilling witnesses, before they could draw breath, but not before a low indignant outcry, "No, no!" had burst from the young doctor's lips. She turned upon him with the speed of lightning. "Mr. Darrell!" she cried, "was it a tramp that got into my child's room in the middle of the night? Speak the truth before God!"

What did she suspect or fear? The question flashed through his mind with a shock of strange sensation. "No," he said, looking at her, "it was no tramp."

"And you know who it was?"

She rose up and confronted him with her pale, set face, holding him with her eyes, which were like Hetty's eyes, in the strain of the horrible gaze that had settled in them that night. He was helpless in her hands like a child. "Yes," he said, "I know."

She could not speak, but she made him an imperative gesture to go on. He was no longer the unwilling witness, he was the conscious criminal at the bar.

"Mrs. Asquith," he said, with a shiver of nervous emotion, "it needs a long explanation. I would have to tell you many things to make you understand."

"Many things which you have no right to tell any one, Mr. Darrell," the housekeeper said.

Mary once more insisted with an imperious wave of her

126

hand. The young man made a nervous pause. "I have an—invalid gentleman under my charge," he said.

"Mr. Darrell!" cried the housekeeper again, "do you remember all you've promised? You've no right to go against them that support you, them that pay you."

"What is that to me?" cried Mary quickly. "What do I want with your secrets? Tell me about my child!"

"I will tell you everything," he said. "It has been against my conscience always. I'll have this burden no longer. He wanders about at night, we can't help it, he slips from our hands. And I suppose he saw the open window. I—I was too late to keep him back. I found him there. He thought she was his child, whom he thinks he has lost. When I heard her scream I knew how it was, and I got him away."

"Is this the truth?" Mrs Asquith said; "is this all the truth?"

"It is everything," cried the young man; "there is nothing more to tell you, but there is more for me to do. I give up this charge, Mrs. Mills. I will do it no more, it is against my conscience. If he only knew a little better he could bring us both up for conspiracy. I will clear my conscience of it this very day."

"If you are such a fool!" the housekeeper said in her excitement. She went round to him and caught him by the arm, and led him aside, talking eagerly. "She'll pay no attention. What does she care for anything but her girl?" the woman said.

Mary had seated herself again suddenly, her brain swimming, her heart beating. Thank God! she said to herself. She did not know what she had feared, but something more dreadful, worse than this; her relief was greater than words could say. She sat down to recover herself. What the housekeeper said was true. She cared for nothing but her girl. What were their secrets to her? If somebody was wronged Mary did not feel that it was her business to set it right. It was her child or whom, and of whom alone, she was thinking; and in all probability no further thoughts of the mysterious invalid would have crossed her mind, but for this incident which now occurred, and which for the moment was nothing but an annoyance to her, detaining her from Hetty. There was a knock at the door, to which the others in their preoccupation paid no attention. After a second knock the door was softly opened, and one of the women servants came in, a tidy person, in the dark gown and white cap and apron, which is a respectable maid-servant's livery. She hesitated for a moment, and then said, "Oh, please, is Mrs. Asquith here?"

"Yes, I am here," cried Mary, quickly getting up, with the idea that she was being called to Hetty. The woman came in,

127

hurried forward, and made curtsey after curtsey—a little sniff of suppressed crying attending each—"Oh, ma'am, don't you know me? Oh, ma'am, I've never forgotten you! Oh, please, I am Bessie Brown," she said.

"Are you indeed Bessie Brown? I am very glad to see you," said Mrs. Asquith. "And are you here in service? And how is it I never heard about you from my Hetty? You were the first nurse she ever had."

"Oh, ma'am, is that our baby? and me never to know! I never heard her name right. I never knew. Oh, to think that poor young lady is our baby! And the dreadful, dreadful fright she got! But oh! ma'am, perhaps now you've come it is all for the best."

"How can it be for the best that my child should be so ill?" said Mary. "Oh, she is so ill! To see her is enough to break one's heart."

And in the softness of this sympathy, the first touch of the old naturalness and familiarity which she had yet felt, Mary too began to cry in the fulness of her heart.

"The house is dreadful changed, ma'am, and everything going wrong, I think, though it mayn't be a servant's place to speak."

"I am afraid," Mrs. Asquith said, "I am selfish. I think too much of my own. I can't enter into the troubles of the new family. It's only of the old I can think when I am here."

"But oh! it's no new family, ma'am; it's the same family, it's your own, own family," cried Bessie Brown. "If you're married ever so, you can't give your natural relations up."

"My natural relations!" Mary cried.

But the conversation by this time had caught the watchful ear of the housekeeper, who left Darrell and came back to see what was going on here.

"Brown," she said, "what are you doing in this room? who told you to come and talk to a lady who is paying a visit in the house? I hope, Mrs. Asquith, you'll excuse her. There is no rudeness meant," the housekeeper said.

"My natural relations," Mary repeated. "I don't know what you mean. The house has passed into other hands. I don't suppose there are any of my relations here."

"Brown, you had better go to your work. I'll answer the lady's questions. We did not know till the other day that there was any relationship."

"But," said Mary bewildered, "it is Mrs. Rotherham——"

"Mrs. Prescott-Rotherham. My lady was an heiress. She married Mr. Prescott——"

128

The discovery was too bewildering and strange to convey itself distinctly to Mary's troubled brain. She said only something which she felt to be entirely irrelevant.

"Who, then, is the invalid gentleman?" she cried.

CHAPTER XXIII

THE SICK-ROOM

MRS. ASQUITH took her place in Hetty's room to keep watch there, with indescribable anxiety and alarm. She had been warned that every night since that mysterious occurrence Hetty had seemed to go over again in her dreams the midnight visit which had jarred her being. It had been the effort of her nurses to soothe and silence her, to get her, if possible, to forget; but every night the dreadful recollection had come back. Mary sat down to watch, feeling that this moment of return upon the cause of all the trouble might be the moment of recovery, if she but knew how to use it aright. But that was the question, of far more importance for the moment than those other wonders and anxieties which had arisen in her mind, and which she had not been able to satisfy. How was she to act that this moment might be the critical one, that she might be able to penetrate within the mist that enveloped Hetty? She tried to think, tried to form for herself a plan of action, but with trembling and doubt. The child's life, the child's reason, might depend upon her own presence of mind, her power to touch the right chord, her wisdom. Mary had never taken credit to herself for wisdom. She had never had to face the intricate problems of human consciousness; how to minister to a mind diseased had never been among her many duties. Out of all the simple calls of her practical life, out of her nursery, where everything was so innocent, how was she to reach at once to the height of such a crisis as this? She tried to apply all her unused faculties to it; but they eluded her, and ran into frightened anticipations, endeavours to realise what was about to happen. She had no confidence that she would keep her self-possession, or have her wits about her when the moment come. Oh, if Harry had but been here! But then she remembered all he had to do, and was glad to think that he would be quietly asleep and unconscious of what was going on; and that after all, the fatigue, and the disquietude and dreadful fear that she would not be equal to the necessities of the occasion, would be endured by herself alone. He had plenty to trouble him, she reflected. He would be wretched enough in his anxiety, without wishing him to share this vigil. And then Mary appealed silently to the only One Who is never absent in trouble, imploring Him to stand by her; and felt a little relief in that, and in the softening tears that came with her prayer.

The room was very still, and so was the house, all wrapt in sleep and silence. The housekeeper and Miss Hofland had both offered to sit up, but she had rejected all companionship. She could not have borne the presence of a stranger, or the possibility of any third person coming between her and her child. A nightlight burned faintly in a corner; the light of the fire diffused a soft glow. All was warm and still and breathless in the deep quiet of the night. And as the hours passed on so still, bringing no change with them, Mary's thoughts wandered to the past, into which she seemed to have come back when she entered this house. Her youth seemed to come back: the familiar figures which she had not seen for years surrounded her once more. Hetty slept, or seemed to sleep, not moving in her bed; and in Mary's thoughts the familiar room took back its old appearance. This was where the mother of the house had sat with her basket of coloured worsteds and her endless work, which was never done. And there the girls had their little establishments: Anna with her music, Sophie with her little drawings. Neither the drawings nor the music had been of high quality, but Mary's anxious heart went away to them in the midst of this vigil, and got a moment's refreshment and affectionate soft consolation out of their faded memory. She had not been of much account in those days, but they had all been good to her. And now they were both at the other end of the world, knowing nothing of Mary, as Mary knew nothing of them. And Percy, where was he, the handsome, careless fellow? And John, poor John? Ah! that struck a different chord in her musings. Where was he, if this house was still his? and who was the wife that had made him rich, and then left him, and left her child in this mysterious way? Where was John? Was it true that he had lost his wits (he had so few, dear fellow, at the best of times!), and was shut up somewhere in a madhouse, as had been said? Shut up in a madhouse, he who never would have hurt a fly, shut up—shut up!

Mary's thoughts had run away with her, had made her forget for a moment what was her chief object, her only object. The start she gave, when a new and alarming idea thus came into her mind, brought her back to herself. She had drifted towards that wondering suspicion, that undefined alarm on the evening before, after Bessie's revelation, and Mrs. Mills' evident desire to stave off all further questions. Who was the invalid gentleman? she had asked with an awakening of curiosity, of interest, and wonder. But the housekeeper and the doctor had been called most opportunely away, and she had got no answer to a question. She started when it came back thus in sudden overwhelming force. But the very keenness of the question, which felt almost like a discovery, brought her back to herself with a guilty sensation, as if she had forgotten Hetty in thus following out another train of thought. And what was all the world in comparison with Hetty, whose well-being now hung in the balance, and whom perhaps her mother, dreaming and thinking of others, might miss the moment to save? She recovered herself in an instant, and brought herself back with all her mind concentrated upon her child. Hetty lay still as in depths of sleep; but from time to time her eyes were opened, though only to close again, and the sight of those open eyes chilled the mother through and through, and drove everything else out of her mind. It was now the most ghostly depth of night, the darkest and the coldest, when morning seems to begin to wake with a chill and shiver. Hetty's eyes had closed again, and Mrs. Asquith had resumed her seat to watch, with a nervous anticipation of the crisis—when presently the bed shook with the nervous shuddering of the little form that lay on it; and starting up, she found Hetty with her eyes wide open, an agonised look upon her face, and her hands clutching the bedclothes, as had been described to her. The mother's dress brushing the bed as she rose hastily, seemed to increase the dreamer's horror. She began to move from side to side, moaning as in a nightmare, struggling to rise. And then a babble of broken words came to her lips. What was she saying? Mrs. Asquith listened with keen anguish, her faculties sharpened to their utmost strain. Was it some explanation, some complaint, that Hetty was trying to utter, something that would make this mystery clear? Her mother made out that it was the same thing over and over, now more now less clear. Her ears made out the words at last by dint of repetition—Heaven knows, the most innocent words!—"My child, my little darling! my child, my little darling! have I found you at last?"

When this had gone on for some time, Mary in her excitement could bear it no longer. She raised her child suddenly in her arms, clasping her close, taking possession of her in a transport of love and pity. "Hetty!" she cried, "Hetty!" almost with a shriek. "What is it? what is it? Tell me what it is!"

The girl uttered another cry, a wild and piercing shriek, as shrill as that which on the former occasion had roused the house. She started up in her bed, struggling, pushing Mrs. Asquith's arms away, looking wildly round her with the frantic gaze of terror. Then all at once the contrast seemed to reach her stunned soul—not darkness and the awful visitant who had driven her out of herself, but light and that beloved face which poor Hetty thought she had not seen for years. She gave another cry of recognition, "Mother!" and flung herself upon her mother's breast. Mrs.

132

Asquith trembled with the shock, for Hetty plunged into her arms and buried her face as if she had fled into some place of refuge; but if it had been the weight of the great house, as well as that of Hetty, Mary could have borne it in the sudden hope and relief of her soul.

"My dearest!" she said, "my sweet, my own Hetty, I'm here. There's nobody can touch you, I'm here! Don't you know, my darling, your mother? There's nobody can touch you while I am here!"

Hetty made no response in words, but she suspended her whole weight upon her mother, clinging to her, burrowing with her head on Mary's bosom. It was no ordinary embrace; it was the taking of sanctuary, the entry into a city of refuge. So far as the child was aware, she had found her natural protector for the first time. She hid herself in Mary, disappearing almost in the close clasping arms, in the soft shield and shelter of her mother's form. Mary's head was bowed down on Hetty's; her shoulders curved about her; the girl's slim white figure almost disappeared, all pressed, folded, enclosed in the mother's embrace. This was what the housekeeper saw when she rushed to the door, roused by the scream, expecting some repetition of the former scene. Mary signed to her with her eyes, having no other part of her free, to go away. She made the same sign to Miss Hofland, who appeared in her nightdress, trembling and distressed, behind the well-clothed housekeeper. Mary felt that she dared not speak to them, dared not even move or say a word. The success of all depended on her being left alone with her child.

Even the movement of this interruption, however, though hushed and full of precaution, aided the clearing of Hetty's brain. She raised her head for a moment, gave a furtive glance round. "Is he—is he—gone, mamma?"

"Yes, my darling; there is no one here but you and I."

Hetty moved a little more, and cast a tremulous glance, holding her mother tighter and tighter, over her shoulders. "Is the window—shut? Is it safe? Are you sure? Are you sure"—with another passionate strain, under which Mary tottered, yet held up mechanically, she could not tell how—"that he can't come back?"

To Hetty's bewildered mind the terrible moment of that midnight visit had only just passed. She knew nothing of the interval; nor did she ask how it was that, miraculously, when she was most wanted, her mother had come to her; that is always natural in a child's experience. She wanted no explanation of that, but only to make sure that the cause of her terror had disappeared.

"Darling, lie down and go to sleep. You are safe, quite safe. I am going to stay with you, don't you see? Could any harm happen to you and me here?"

Hetty raised her head and turned her face upward for her mother's kiss. It was warm and soft with returning life. "No!" she said, with a long-drawn breath, with that profound conviction of childhood. She had turned into a child after her trance, all other development disappearing for the moment. But her hands seemed incapable of disengaging themselves. She could not loosen her hold. "Oh, mamma, don't let me go! oh, hold me fast! Oh, don't let any one come, mamma!"

"Nobody, my love; I won't leave you, not for a moment—not for a moment, Hetty."

After a while the girl fell fast asleep, with her head upon her mother's shoulder, and her arms so soft, yet clenched like iron round Mary's neck. Hetty was far too profoundly dependent, too desperate in her absolute need, to be capable of thinking of the comfort of her shield and guardian. Cramped and aching, but happy and relieved beyond description in mind, Mary, too, after a while dozed and slept. When she opened her eyes, the chill grey of the morning was coming on. The night was over, with its dangers and fears. Hetty's desperate clinging had relaxed; her head was falling back; the soft warmth and ease of sleep had softened all the rigidity of her trance away. Mary laid her down softly upon her pillow with a light heart, though every limb and every muscle was aching, and took her place once more by the bedside, that she might be the first object on which her child's waking eyes should rest. And Hetty slept—how long she slept! Fatigue crept over Mrs. Asquith; she dozed, and dreamed, and woke with a start, half-a-dozen times before, in the full daylight, Hetty opened her eyes. There was a moment of awful suspense—the blank look of her stupefied state seemed to waver for an instant over her face, like a mist trembling, wavering, uncertain whether to go or stay. Then light broke out, and love and meaning in the girl's eager look. "Oh, mamma!"

There had been by this time many anxious tappings at the door. Miss Hofland had looked in with an anxious face; and little Rhoda, with eyes full of awe, had peeped round the edge of the door; and the housekeeper, with whispers and signs and that invariable cup of tea which is intended to be the consolation of the watcher. But Mary would not be beguiled for a moment from her child's side; the danger was too near, the deliverance too great, to be trifled with. And the other great questions which had almost distracted her mind from Hetty came back as she waited. Hetty's murmurs in the hour of recollection had strangely, fantastically

134

strengthened her suspicions. Could she dare to recall Hetty, waking and restored to reason, to that awful remembrance? Whatever happened she could not risk her child.

This question was put to rest later in the day by Hetty herself, who, very weak, scarcely able to move with physical exhaustion, lay still in her bed, regarding her mother with all a child's beatitude. She had heard all the nursery stories again, Rhoda assisting as before, and laughed and cried and been happy in all the sweetness of convalescence over the little witticisms of baby. But later, when Rhoda, was sent away, Hetty lay very silent for a time, and then called her mother to her bedside.

"Mamma," she said, growing paler and deeply serious, "I wanted to ask you, could he take me for Rhoda? Could he be— could he be—Rhoda's father, mamma?"

"Hetty," said Mary, taking her child's hands, "could you repeat to me, my darling, quietly, without exciting yourself, what you told me in the night? What he said?"

The colour came in a flood to Hetty's face, then ebbed away, leaving her quite pale. She clasped her mother's hands tight; and then she repeated slowly, like a lesson, "Oh, my child, my little darling! have I found you at latht?"

"Oh, Hetty! God bless you, my dearest! Why did you say 'at latht'?" Mary cried.

Hetty looked at her mother with startled eyes. "I don't know what I said. I said only what he said, mamma."

"Hetty," cried Mary in great agitation, "I think God has sent us here, both you and me."

135

CHAPTER XXIV

THE INVALID GENTLEMAN

MARY stole out in the afternoon, when the day was beginning to wane. It was not only that as soon as her anxieties were relieved the spell of the old associations came back: a far more serious pre-occupation was in her mind, though all was mystery round her. The question that had sprung up within her came back and back like a fitful wind through all the agitations and happiness of the day. Her body was altogether worn out by excitement and anxiety, and by the long vigil of that troubled night; but, as happens sometimes in such a case, her mind was only the more eager and alive, her senses keener to everything around. She had sat by Hetty's bedside and talked all the day, talked till her throat and breast seemed to be strained with physical exertion, talked against time, against weariness, that her child's mind might be filled with the peaceful image of home, so as to leave no room for those distracting images which had jarred her whole being. Mary felt the strain of that monologue almost more than any other form of fatigue. She was well used to it, as to all other forms of exhaustion. Talking to children both her own and others, telling stories, giving lessons, the sensation was not new to her; but it made the silence and sweet air very grateful, as, leaving Hetty once more asleep, with Miss Hofland established at her bedside, she stole out into the great quiet of nature, into the dewy park and wonderful serenity of the spring afternoon, as it began to soften into night.

The grass had been growing all day, the flowers struggling, making their way upward, the young leaves unrolling their tightly-bound folds out of their sheaths; and now all seemed to have paused in the midst of that hopeful, cheerful progress, to rest a little, to get strength for a warmer effort still. Life, all thrilling through the awakened earth in every vein, in every pore, paused in the midst of that warm impulse to rest. She felt in sympathy with all the world, delivered from a terror beyond description,—from death, and worse than death, her very exhaustion adding to the refreshment and blessedness of that quiet and repose. For the moment, except for a vague sense in her mind of an uneasiness which she held at arm's length, she was able to give herself up entirely to this tranquil sweetness. She wandered out, going round the old house, with every line of which her eyes were familiar, the dear old house, about which she had tripped in her childhood, when she had been "only Mary," running everybody's errands, doing what everybody told her—a little unconsidered happy creature, sent up and down, here and there, but never unkindly, never untenderly, she said to herself with tears in her eyes. Oh, never unkind! nothing but a little wholesome neglect, the carelessness of familiarity which in its way was sweet. She had not been like her own children, wrapped in love from their cradles, their little interests and pleasures put above everything; but Mary knew that she had been as happy as a lamb or a bird—creatures which have no special tendance, but to which all nature is sweet. She had never known what harsh words were, or harsh judgments. They had let her grow like a flower; they had kept her from the colds and from the heats of life; covered her and sheltered her, and loved her in their way. She looked back upon her young life with a tender gratitude, more profound than if they had made her the chief object. She had not been so to any one in Horton, but how much more, she said to herself, in consequence, all their sweetness and kindness was. To make your own child happy, upon whom your happiness depends, what is that but selfishness of the most refined kind? But to make a little creature happy upon whom your happiness does not depend—is not that true love, the charity of the Gospel? She thought of them all who had been so good to her, so kind, so careless, so indulgent, her heart swelling with tenderness and gratitude.

When she had got far enough off to take in the full view of the house, she turned back, renewing as it were her acquaintance with it, following with tender recollection every line and curve. It was changed in some respects. The front of the house had been renovated, some parts of the architecture carefully restored, the grounds about the house all put into luxurious order. Altogether, she said to herself, it looked as if a wave of prosperity had visited the place, as if there were no longer a deficiency of gardeners or of servants to keep it in perfection, as there once was. The lawn looked as if it were rolled every day; there was no sign of neglect anywhere—and once there had been so many signs. Only one thing in which there was no change met her eyes. The east wing was all shut up as of old, the windows closely shuttered, every opening closed. All the same, and yet a little different. In former days it had been evidently a natural expedient, the shutting up of a portion of the house which the family was not numerous enough or wealthy enough to keep up. Now it was different. It was an obvious breach of the wealthy propriety of the place, about which there was no indication that such an expedient could be necessary. Mary walked slowly round that side of the house. The shutting up even was not as before. It was far more elaborate, done with precaution, as if with the view of closing the interior from all inspection. In the old times, no one had minded what loop-hole there might be; appearances had not been thought of. And then her heart began to beat loudly in her ears. Was it possible that this was a prison, a place of confinement? and who was it that was shut up there?

Who was it that could be shut up there? By what right or wrong, without warrant or authority, nobody knowing, nobody able to help! All the questions that had been in Mary's mind, suspended by her exhaustion, and by the grateful quiet of which she had so much need, sprang up again in the fullest force. The strange words which Hetty had murmured in her trance, which she had repeated when in full possession of her mind, which had evidently engraved themselves on her brain, and which had roused her mother to one sudden gleam of enlightenment, came back to her again and seemed to echo in her ears. She had put them away after that first impression. How could it be? Why should it be? In those days such things could not happen. Shut up the master of the house in his own habitation, separate him from his child, conceal him from the world! How could it be? Who could do it? The motives and the means seemed both wanting. But Mary's brain throbbed and whirled, even as she said all this to herself. She forgot even Hetty in the gathering excitement of her mind. She walked up and down, up and down, at the foot of the grassy slope on which those barricaded windows opened. Yes, they had always been barricaded, but not as they were now!

The night began to darken round her; already the shrubberies, the distant trees in the park, began to grow indistinct. The veil of the twilight dropped slowly over the brightness of the sky. But Mary took no notice; her steps made no sound upon the damp and mossy velvet of the turf; her mind grew every moment less under her own control. What could she do to satisfy that question? Was he there? Who was he? What could she do? She was but a stranger, though a child of the house; she had nothing to prove that the invalid gentleman of whom the doctor had spoken, the wanderer who had broken in upon her child's rest, had in reality any connection with the family, or was one for whom she could interfere: and how could she interfere?—a stranger, a poor woman, the mother of Miss Rotherham's companion. That was all Mary was to the servants and people about. And the invalid might be a stranger too, for anything she could tell; he might be—anyone. What right had she to jump to a conclusion, and decide thus who he was? But she could not go in quietly and sit down, and take care of her child, and perhaps sleep, while all the while, close to her, within her reach, might be shut up, deprived of everything, one who perhaps was the rightful master of all. But how could that be? How could that be? Why, and with what motive, could such a thing be done? Her brain turned round more than ever, her mind was all confused, hanging in the misery of doubt and helplessness, suspended between the how and the why.

Suddenly she heard a stealthy sound behind her, as of an opened window or door. She was at the end of the slope, and turned round quickly at this indication of some one moving. At the end of the long range of windows she saw a head put dimly forth, and then disappear. Mary divined that it was her own appearance, vague as it must be in the twilight, which was the cause. She changed her position, rapidly concealing herself behind a clump of laurels, and waited. After a little interval there was a faint stir once more. Almost afraid to breathe, she looked out between the thick leaves. Something had come out into the dimness of the night. She felt only as Hetty had done, a movement, a something that was human, a new breathing in the still atmosphere. The leaves rustled now and then in the night air, and she felt as if it must be she who did it, and put her hands upon the bough to keep them still. A strange horror, half superstitious, came over her; something was coming without any sound, with nothing but a consciousness in the tingling atmosphere. She forgot the yielding of the turf, in which no footstep was audible. It seemed to her that something incorporate, some vision sensible to the mind alone, must be moving past unseen. Terror took possession of her soul. Was it this then, and not any suffering human creature, some one who had come back, some one out of the darkness of the grave, whose presence should chill the blood in her veins, as he had chilled her child's. Mary felt as if she hung by her hands from the laurel boughs, which she had grasped to keep them still. Then, with a sensation of utter horror, she felt herself slip from them, her hands relaxing. It had passed; her heart stood still; the surging blood went up and up in blinding circles to her brain. Then there was a sudden calm in her being, and the common action of life was taken up again in a moment. In front of her, going softly across the dim lawn, was a long slim shadow, the head bent a little, the gait uncertain, swaying as if with weakness. Mary's superstitious terrors had vanished in a moment. It was a man she saw; who he was no one could have told, in the faint evening, on the noiseless grass; but at all events it was a man.

Mary's faculties all came back. Suppose the guess she had made was right, suppose it was he, with only herself in all the world to protect him! She disengaged herself from the bushes, and gliding from one shelter to another, sometimes dropping to the ground in her terror, lest he should be alarmed and fly from her, she followed. The night was soft and dim, wrapping all things in a ghostly shadow; but she never lost sight of the vague, moving thing winding out and in among the bushes, avoiding with a kind of strange skill the front of the house. He made a long round, and Mary kept up mechanically, always following, her limbs failing under her. When he had got round to the other side, he drew slowly near to the corresponding range of windows in the western wing; and after various falterings mounted the slope, and made his way along close to the house. The faltering, stealthy figure stealing along, now with a foot upon the ledge of stone, now all noiseless upon the turf, made her half shudder with terror, notwithstanding the excitement, which was all of which she was now sensible, the only thing that kept her up. Should anyone within catch a glimpse of the noiseless shadow thus stealing round the house, what wonder if panic and maddening terror should follow his steps! Mary, stumbling on, felt that she was going through all that was preliminary to that midnight visit which had half crazed her child. The gliding figure suddenly stopped. She saw it pause, turn inward, put up two arms to the window. Thank God, it was no longer Hetty's window; the child was safe. And once more, once more—by what chance who could tell?—the opening gave way. With a last effort of strength pulling herself together, Mary climbed the slope.

It had become so dark without that the night had seemed far advanced, but within lights were shining. The door of the room stood open, admitting a cheerful glimmer; the sound of voices was audible. Mary came quickly in, shutting the window behind her, her excitement risen to fever point. She found herself confronting the ghostly figure, which stood bewildered in the middle of the room. Even now, even here, sure as she was that it was a man, and a helpless one, who stood before her, the horrible alternative, the wild suggestion, that at her touch that shadow might dissolve and melt away, and leave her mad with the awful encounter, flashed through Mary's confused brain. To stand by him in the dark room was somehow more appalling than to follow through the free air and space. But it was only in that flash that she remembered herself at all. The poor wanderer had known his way when he was making that devious course round the house: he had come soberly with an evident intention through the clumps and bosquets to this window—he had meant all along to get here, to enter by it, to pursue his wild search for his child. But the open door on the other side, the lights gleaming, the sounds of the household, all active and awake, bewildered him. He stopped short; perhaps he had already seen that there was no one in the bed. He stood wavering, tremulous, diverted from his intention, looking wildly round him. When he caught sight of Mary he shrank back, as if to escape. Trembling as she was, her lips almost refusing to utter the words that came to them, her limbs to support her, she tottered up to him, and caught him by the arm.

"Yes," he said, retreating a little before her. "Don't be angry—I wanted to thee my little girl."

"Oh, John!" cried Mary. "Cousin John!—oh, dear John, you that were always so good, why won't they let you live as you ought in your own house?"

He stepped still further back, with a gesture of dismay. "Who is that?" he said. "You're not Mrs. Mills. I don't know who you are."

"Oh yes, John, you know me, if you will only think; I'm Mary. You remember Mary, your little cousin, to whom you were always so good?"

"Mary?" he said. "I know your voice, and I know your name: but they will not like it. They thay I'm not fit—Mary—I wonder if I would know you if I thaw you. But don't tell them I'm here; I daren't go into the light."

"Cousin John," said Mary, "tell me who you think I am."

He drew back a little farther; it seemed to bewilder him to be so near her. "I think," he said, "you must be little Mary that used to be at home in the old time, Mary that wath married to the curate. I wath very found of Mary. But don't tell them I'm here. I'll go back—I'll go back—to my own little place."

"This is your place, John. Oh, dear John, who has done this to you? You shall not go back; you shall stay in your own house, John."

"It will only get you into trouble," he said in a dreamy tone. "She thaid—she told me——" his voice ran off into a murmur of sound; perhaps the effect of that she, which he uttered with a sharp sibilation, was too much for him; or perhaps the thought of her was too much. "Perhapth I had better go back."

"No," cried Mary, grasping his arm with both her hands. "Come with me and see your little girl."

"Oh, my little girl: my little darling!" the poor fellow cried, and resisted no more.

141

CHAPTER XXV

THE RESTORATION

RHODA'S sitting-room was very warm and pleasant and quiet, the safest and most comfortable place—the fire lighting it up with fitful gleams, the windows still glimmering between the curtains with the dim twilight which had not turned to dark, the pictures and mirrors on the walls giving forth gleams of ruddy reflection. There were no longer flowers outside to brighten the prospect, but within groups of plants in every corner, and a tall pot of creamy, fragrant narcissus spreading its delicate spring scent through the room. The warm flicker of the firelight seemed to draw out the sweetness of the flowers, the deeper tints of colour, the reds and browns of the furniture. There could not have been a woman's apartment more entirely breathing of women, and of comfort, and tranquillity, and peace. Hetty lay on the sofa near the fire, the ruddy glow shedding a pink colour over her still pale face. Rhoda sat at her feet, leaning against the sofa, holding up her eager little face, asking questions in her eager way about Hetty's home, about the children, about baby, who was so funny. "Oh! I wish I could see him. Oh, I wish I could go and play with them all!" Rhoda said. Hetty, who had been removed here in her mother's absence to join the little party once more, in the sweetness of that convalescence, which was almost more than coming back to health, lay smiling, answering the child's questions in a little broken voice of weakness and happiness. Miss Hofland sat on a low chair by the fire, going through her usual little calculations, setting down all the comforts on one side against the very curious condition of this house on the other. All these things that had happened were very mysterious. The whispers of the maids, which could scarcely fail to reach her, were full of suggestions. It was not pleasant to live in a house where such strange things were heard and seen; but then, on the other hand, it was very comfortable. There was scarcely anything one wanted that one could not have. In some families the treatment was very different. She was putting these things meditatively against one another when the servant came in with the lamp. There was an abundant supply of light, as of everything else—no stint of anything—lamps and candles, it did not seem to matter how many were used. It was very comfortable, enough to make up for the many unpleasant circumstances which did not after all touch either her pupil or herself.

142

Just then the servant, going away after he had placed the lamp, uttered a cry of alarm, and seemed to fall back against the wall, letting go the handle of the door. Miss Hofland started up, feeling that if anything dreadful came in here, into this warm and pleasant place, all the comfort would not make up for such an interruption. She rose so hurriedly that her chair turned over, coming down with a muffled sound on the carpet, and turned her startled face towards the door. Mrs. Asquith had just come in, looking very pale and excited, leaning upon the arm of—no, she was not leaning, she was guiding him with her hand through his arm—a tall, slim man with a strange grey coat, too large for him, and wrapping over his shadowy thinness, a long face, with large projecting eyes, grizzled hair hanging wildly, a ragged beard, and drooping, melancholy moustache hiding the outlines of the tremulous mouth. He had a bewildered, dazed look, and turned his head slowly from side to side, as if he scarcely saw, and did not know where he was.

And before a word could be said, almost before the attention of the girls had been roused, or Miss Hofland's cry of alarm got vent, the housekeeper rushed into the room. She swept into it like a whirlwind, and placed herself at the other side of that strange figure.

"Sir, sir!" she cried, "you must go back, you must go back—you must not be seen here!"

"John!" cried Mrs. Asquith, "don't give way to her; this is your house, and here is your child."

He turned his face from one side to the other, shrinking a little from the housekeeper, yet making a step back as if in obedience—appealing to Mary, yet drawing his arm away from hers in a self-contradictory movement, opening his mouth but only with a gasp, saying nothing.

Mrs. Mills put her hand upon his sleeve.

"Come back, sir," she said; "come back, oh! come back to your own comfortable room, where things are fit and proper for you. My mistress would break her heart if she thought you were here. Oh, sir, come back! You know what my mistress would say, and that it's all for your good. What does she think of night and day but for your good?"

He gasped again as if for breath, and then drew away, retreating a little. "Mary," he said, "perhapth she's right. I'll be better in my own place." As he stood thus irresolute, feeble, with a woman on each side of him, a picture of a bewildered soul cowed with long subjection, there came into the movement of the strange little drama another unexpected actor. Hetty had sprung up from her sofa, forgetting her weakness, putting out her hands at first as if to keep away the sight; and her movement had disturbed Rhoda, who sprang up too, and stood for a moment astonished, taking in the scene. Then with a cry the little girl flung herself forward, clutching at the grey coat, clinging to his knees. "Father!" she cried. Her little voice, shrill in its childish tones, rang through the air like the ring of a pistol shot, clearing away the mist. He gave a great, sobbing cry, shook himself clear, and stooping down, gathered the child into his arms. They all stood round, a group of hushed spectators, to watch that meeting. He seemed to grope for a chair, and sat down and folded her to him. "My little girl, my darling! my little girl, my darling! I've found you at latht!" Hetty tottered across the floor to her mother, and caught her arm and clung to her, hiding her head upon Mary's shoulder. And behind them all young Darrell came in, and stood looking on like the rest.

Even the housekeeper had been paralysed by this touching sight; she had not been able to speak or interfere, but at the appearance of Darrell she recovered herself. "Doctor," she said, going up to him, "you know what our orders are, you know he'll hurt himself by this, you know it's for his good—for his good. What were we put here for but for his good? And who is this lady that has ventured to interfere? Doctor, call Turner, call the man, and take him back. I order you," cried the woman, "in my mistress's name, take him back. Sir, sir, Mr. Prescott! take the child from him, take him back."

No one paid any attention to her cries, and the woman was almost beside herself. "Miss Hofland," she said, "it's as much as our places are worth. You said yourself it was a comfortable house. Oh, for goodness' sake take the child from him, take the child from him! Don't you know he's off his head? I've got my mistress's authority. Turner—doctor—this moment, he must be taken back!"

Little Rhoda here released herself from her father's arms. She put herself before him like a guardian spirit, not angel, for her eyes flashed fire, and her little hands clenched. "If you touch him I'll kill you! I'll kill you!" cried the little girl, setting her white teeth.

"Mrs. Mills," said Mary, "the time for all that is over; I am here to protect my cousin. Whatever your mistress may do or say, I am his nearest relation here. We can take care of Mr. Prescott without you; he shall neither be shut up nor coerced again. Doctor, he knows us all; he only wants his child; he is as gentle as an infant. Why should he be shut up and banished from the light of day?"

"There is no reason at all," young Darrell said. "I am

144

ashamed of my part in it. It was I who opened the door to him to-night; I hoped that this would happen which has happened. I don't know if you will ever believe that I acted at first in good faith. There is no reason, no reason at all, for keeping him confined now."

John Prescott sat holding his child with one arm round her, looking out solemnly upon the group about him. There was something in the aspect of his large immovable eyes, showing that he saw imperfectly if at all, which strangely heightened the effect of the scene. He put out his other arm as if feeling for some one. "Mary, Mary! Wasn't Mary here?"

She came up to him and took his hand. "Yes, John, I am here, I am here: nobody shall touch you. They daren't touch you while I am here."

It was the second time in twenty-four hours that she had brought peace and security by these words—she, a helpless woman, the poor parson's wife, never of much account in the world—and yet they were true! But probably John Prescott did not make any question to himself how that was, or even understand clearly what she was doing for him. He grasped her hand, making no reply to what she said. "Mary," he said slowly, "I want your advice."

"Yes, John."

"Mutht a man do all his wife says? She's clever, and I'm not. I never was one of the clever fellowths. She's gone away, and I promithed—But, Mary, I want my little girl."

"Yes, John, and you shall have her. You shall not be parted again," Mary cried with tears.

"I want my little girl. They say I frightened thome one that wasn't mine; I ask her pardon, I'm sure. I never meant to frighten any one; all I want ith my little girl."

"Father, here I am!" cried little Rhoda, one arm clasping his, one uplifted in defence.

"And, Cousin John, oh! I love you too: I wasn't frightened," Hetty cried.

The sound of this prodigious falsehood, told with all the conviction of the heart, brought a note of something like laughter into the room, when this scene ended, the strange little drama, which, but for Hetty's fright and Mary's arrival, might have been a tragedy, and ended in a very different way.

The explanation of the circumstances was not difficult to give. John Prescott had married, or rather, to use a juster phraseology, had been married to, a Californian lady with a great fortune, who had come to England to dazzle the old civilization, as so many do. But the earl, or the viscount, or the duke's son, who are the natural prey of such conquering invaders, had not turned up, and the beautiful old house, and the armorial bearings of the Prescotts, and all that was old and traditionary about them, had been felt by Miss Rotherham to be next best. To say that her husband belonged to the old untitled aristocracy, who looked upon new lordships with contempt, was so refined and exquisite a piece of brag that the imagination of the daughter of the wilds was captivated by it. And John looked every inch an effete aristocrat, languid with over-civilization. She took him, with his old place and impoverished estate, as if he had been a choicer piece of antiquated lumber than all the rest. But when she had been married for a few years to John, that vivacious representative of the New World had found her stupid Englishman too much for her. His very goodness had driven her frantic. He had submitted to almost anything she exacted, with a dull amiability which took all her patience from her. Finally he had got blind, or almost blind, but never otherwise than patient, uncomplaining, and kind, adoring his child, who adored him, and very submissive to his wife. And she did not find her untitled aristocracy did her much good in a social point of view. The compatriots who had secured the earls and the viscounts laughed, and the Prescotts had fallen out of society too long in the days of their poverty to recover their position easily. And John was dull. Ye heavens! how dull he was—dull even to the simple people who loved him at home—how much more dull to the lively Transatlantic who had intended to build her advancement upon him, but never had loved him at all!

Mrs. Asquith found out by degrees that her cousin's wife had tried to make him out incapable of managing his affairs, and to get him shut up, which was unkind, seeing that he was perfectly content to commit to her hands the management of these affairs, and never grumbled at her absences, or found fault with her proceedings, too happy to be left with Rhoda in the home he loved. Mrs. Prescott-Rotherham, however, had failed in this, and thereupon had organized another plan for freeing herself from circumstances which she would not tolerate. To have great wealth and belong to a new civilization in which there is little bondage of precedent, and not to have whatever you like, whatever you can pay for, is intolerable. It is always intolerable not to be able to do what one pleases, and have what one likes; but these are things which most people have to put up with. Mrs. Prescott-Rotherham did not see why she should put up with anything she disliked so much, and she went off to America to obtain a divorce. If she had told John this, the probabilities were that, unless some sudden gleam of religious objection had crossed the tranquillity of his dulled brain, he would have acquiesced, as he did everything else. But there are limits to the boldness even of a rich Californian, accustomed to see all obstacles disappear before her. And what she did was to persuade her husband that to confine himself entirely to his own rooms would be good for his eyes and for his health, and that until her return it was his policy to lead a secluded life. She pointed out to him the misery of being plagued by visitors, the trouble which even Rhoda's governess would bring upon him, and that to seclude himself in the east wing while she was absent was the best thing he could do. Poor John did not know till she was gone that he was to be secluded from Rhoda too; but though it was very difficult to manage him when he learned this, yet he was smoothed down and coaxed into patience for the time. Needless to say that of the divorce suit going briskly on on the other side of the Atlantic nobody knew. The citation to John to appear had been conveyed to him in a newspaper, which he had solemnly opened, as was his wont, looked at with his half-blind eyes, and put away with the remark that there was nothing in it. He was indeed more than half blind, and the paper conveyed to him no information at all.

It is needless to say that Mrs. Prescott-Rotherham obtained her divorce in the American court, but that the English law, as was natural, took no notice of that decree, and altogether refused to take Rhoda from her father's keeping. It is equally of course that from the moment when Mary led him back into his own house, there could be no question of secluding him any more. He was as sane as he had ever been, understanding everything that was kind and friendly, not wise nor yet abundant in speech, which would have been out of nature. The poor relation, who was only Mary, and the poor parson whom she had married, protected his gentle weakness, and John Prescott, with his patient yet half-tragic face, his almost sightless eyes, and his little story of undeserved wrong, wrong of which even now he was barely conscious, opining that his wife had only gone to visit her relations and meant no harm, made a great impression upon the Commissioners in Lunacy who examined him, and pronounced in his favour authoritatively, adding however a gentle recommendation that in view of his yielding character he should have some relation to stay with and to take care of him. This condition was fulfilled by the return of his sister Anna from India, widowed, shortly after, and thus everything was set right.

Hetty took no harm from that attack, which might have been shortened or even averted if any one had been as bold as her mother. Mr. Darrell was of opinion that she required very careful watching for a long time—watching which the young man was too willing to give. He remained in the position of the family doctor for some time after for this cause, in his anxiety about Hetty's health: and as soon as her parents consider her old enough there is little doubt that he will get his reward.

John Prescott was left poor when his wife, baffled yet emancipated, took away her money, as when the negotiations were all over she was at liberty to do—but without the child, who clung to him, and would not hear a word said of her mother. He was left quite poor, poorer even than the Prescotts had been in Mary's early days. But yet there was something in Cousin John's power. One morning, about a year after, the post brought news of the death of the Rev. Hugh Prescott, the rector of Horton, in one of the villages of the Riviera where he had lived so long. In strict justice the appointment ought to have gone to the old clergyman who had officiated as his locum tenens for a dozen years. But when was strict justice ever regarded in this world? John would receive no council on this matter. He had been pronounced able to manage his own affairs, and in this one point at least he was determined to do so. He tried, in his blindness to write a letter to Mary with his own hands offering the Rectory to her husband. The letter was illegible, but the purpose was carried out, and thus Mary returned with all her children to the home of her youth.

"Don't speak of it, Miss Hetty; don't speak of it," said the old clergyman. "If you think I know so little of the world as to believe that the claims of pure justice, as you call it, could ever stand against the claims of the Squire's cousin—But your father is a good man, and you and your mother have been the saving of the Prescotts, and I don't grudge it, though perhaps it is a little hard upon me."

Everything that is good for one is a little hard perhaps for some one else—or almost everything. Mary thinks sometimes that it is a little hard upon Mrs. Rotherham, once Prescott, to be deprived of her only child; but then, when a woman cannot put up with a dull husband, which is so much less a matter than many other matrimonial burdens, what can she expect? And on the whole, no doubt everything is for the best.